HELL HOUNDS

Heaven and Hell Series Book Two

Barb Jones

Immortal Cravings LLC

CONTENTS

Disclosure	1
Dedication	2
ALSO BY BARB JONES	3
Prologue	4
1	9
2	18
3	28
4	33
5	38
6	43
7	47
8	52
9	57
10	62

11   66

12   71

13   77

14   81

15   85

16   90

17   95

18   100

19   104

20   109

21   113

22   118

23   123

24   127

25   132

26   136

27   143

28   147

29   151

About the Author   155

This book is a work of fiction. Refereces to real people, events, establish-
ments, or locales are intended only to provide a sense of authenticity, and
are used fictitiously. All other characters, and all incidents and dialogue, are
drawn from the author's imagination and are not to be construed as real.

For
Arianna and Kaiden
My personal demon hunters

ALSO BY BARB JONES

blood prophecy series

queen's destiny

queen's enemy

queen's ascension

blood prophecy novellas

amber: birth of a queen

chloe: visions of the future

marcus: origins

machiel: stone of the damned

zaraquel: moral compass

blood prophecy: Dark prophecy series

rise of the hunter

heaven and hell series

son of asmodeus

PROLOGUE

The Child of Destiny

Archangel Michael smiled as Jophiel showed him the child. Michael took the child in his arms, raised him toward the throne, and announced in a firm voice:

"Ecce duorum regnorum filius. Sit laus Domino Deo nostro. Hic puer fatum suum ad Caelum et Infernum implebit."

Michael held the child, and as he gazed into the little one's eyes, he felt a sense of power radiating from him. He smiled, knowing this meant his idea of the agreement between Heaven and Hell had worked. Then he noticed the faintest marking beneath the child's chin—the sign of the pact. Both kingdoms would accept this child.

Turning to Jophiel, he said, "I will take the child to meet Lucifer. I will return. Guard your heart, Jophiel. As you know, he will have limited time with you and his father. He must mature in the human world to safeguard both factions. You have had three days with him. The demon Asmodeus is due his time."

He saw his words sadden Jophiel's face. Michael softened his tone and allowed her to hold her baby for one more small but meaningful moment. Then he departed to meet Lucifer.

Michael stood outside the passage to Hell and called for him. The baby was fussing, which he expected. The passage opened, and the baby's father, the demon prince Asmodeus, appeared alongside Lucifer. Michael showed reverence when addressing the demon, as the pact required, and for the sake of the child. With a nod and a smile, he handed the baby to Prince Asmodeus.

"The kingdom of Heaven has already marked this child. It is time for Hell's kingdom to do likewise. I will return in three days, since he has already spent three days with his mother in Heaven. Guard him well, Lucifer and Prince Asmodeus. He is the child of the pact."

"He's strong, Michael. Look, Lucifer, my liege—he will guard the kingdom of Hell." Asmodeus smiled at his son.

Michael interrupted the tender moment to speak to Lucifer.

"Remember the pact, brother. It binds Heaven and Hell and places this child at the center. Should your legion of demons rise against the pact, or angels from our kingdom rebel, the child's destiny is bound by oath. Neither side can refute it. Death—whether demon or angel—will follow when the child fulfills his destiny."

"I, Lucifer, will honor my part. Don't speak to me like that. I remember our agreement, brother. Or have you forgotten that we share the same Father, Michael?"

After that, Michael gazed at the child with undeniable tenderness before returning to his kingdom. Three days later, he returned to the passage to Hell, calling for Asmodeus and Lucifer. They appeared with the child in his father's arms.

"Three days went by fast. I wonder if his mother felt the same way," Asmodeus said.

"Yes, demon prince. Having a child creates a bond, but raising him in the human world is crucial. It is hard to accept that neither Heaven nor Hell will train him. Lucifer, have you honored the child while he was in Hell? Is he as free to enter your kingdom as he is to enter ours? This is crucial."

Lucifer nodded. "I honored the pact and granted him Hell's protection. His marks will appear when he is ready, and not a moment before. His identity remains unknown to the demons, as the pact requires."

Michael smiled. "I have found the perfect adoptive parents. They will raise him, protect him, and honor his origins. They are aware of his father's and mother's places in the two kingdoms and of his destiny. In time, they will reveal his true birthright and train him under disguise. But duty will constrain him. God has marked him. You have marked him. Lucifer, I will seek you again when the time arrives."

Michael took the child from Asmodeus and returned to Heaven. It was now his turn to protect the boy and bestow his gifts upon him. He considered what the child would need when he became a man. Michael was determined to move forward with the next step of his plan.

England—1537

The bishop approached John while he was kneeling in prayer and interrupted him.

"My son, the gracious King of England bade me seek thee out and deliver into your hands his request. He recognizes demons but does not make it known to his subjects. You shall read this letter and return it to me, so there is no evidence of his request."

John extended his hand for the king's letter. He nodded at the bishop, knowing they shared a private arrangement regarding his unique talents. Seeing the royal seal of King Henry VIII, John tossed it back to the bishop and swore at him.

"Send your master instead of parchment."

The bishop sighed, placed his hand on his neck, and thrust the letter back at John. "Read, my son, for it is better to open the letter than lose our heads."

Demon Hunter:

I shall not ask for your identity but request your aid. The world is full of hellish creatures, including one in my kingdom. I wish to rid our country of this foul-natured beast, but if I were to tell my privy council, they would seek to have me dethroned. Some plot against me still, though I have sat upon the throne for years.

The bishop will share the details of the creature I wish you to hunt. Once the demon is gone, there is another I would have you pursue. There is a heretic in my kingdom. For your loyal service, accept these coins and this unique blade as a token of gratitude—not for me, but for England. I believe you shall find the blade most useful should you have need of it.

King Henry VIII

John waited for the bishop to provide the details once he returned the letter. Hands exchanged parchment for a purse of coins and the blade. After listening carefully, John left the church. He retrieved his sword from the bushes and started back to the room he shared with the demon child while they were in England.

Along the way, he noticed a large, strange-looking dog staring at him with glowing red eyes. Though the animal remained still, John felt pursued by its unblinking gaze. Oddly, he had seen the same dog at different points in his life, though he had never approached it. He disregarded the beast and returned on his way.

Rounding a corner, he collided with a striking woman. Her upward glance revealed demonic features. Her long dark hair spilled down her back, and the dress she wore barely contained her ample chest. She seemed out of place here. Her hand brushed his arm as she whispered, "Son of

Asmodeus," before vanishing. John shrugged, unsettled that he hadn't killed a demon, though he figured it was for the best.

He had heard rumors about the king and had come to England to investigate. While he agreed with some of Henry VIII's positions, he worried for the women the king married. Wandering the countryside, John observed demons living among unsuspecting peasants. He knew his duty, and since the king had asked for his aid, he felt bound to oblige. Demon hunting was his expertise, yet within him stirred a myriad of emotions. Perhaps one day, he would come to understand them.

1

HELL, PRESENT DAY

HELL, PRESENT DAY

Demon princes fought at the council table, discussing recent events with the demon hunter. Balam slammed his fist against the table, demanding silence. Asmodeus sat back and watched tempers flare.

"Silence, fools. The demon hunter had the key when Astaroth fought him last before turning tail and running away. We are demons, not cowards! Then the bastard hunter went silent. He left his apartment, and our demons lost him. We need a plan to control the key."

Astaroth stammered back at him. "Don't blame this on me. The damn hunter became powerful, and Lucifer answered him. It's all Asmodeus' fault. We knew where his true loyalties lay. He was part of the fuckin' pact. We'll overthrow the King of Hell and destroy the pact. Then we enter the kingdom of Heaven and finish what we started ages ago. It's the only way. Plus, Asmodeus brought those women here. He won't let us toy with the pretty women. Especially Katarina. She betrayed us. We should torture the demon bitch back into submission."

Balam interrupted.

"She could be useful to our cause. Isn't that right, Asmodeus?"

Asmodeus stood and snarled in response. "What do you intend to do? The women are under my protection. Discover a different path to reach the hunter."

"Easy now, Asmodeus. We could have Katarina spy on the demon hunter and tell us his progress. Why exert effort when the hunter can do it for us? All you need do is give them to us, and we'll let you overthrow Lucifer yourself. When we agreed to the pact, didn't you desire his power? Why change sides now?"

Asmodeus lost control and glanced at his son Edward, who stood tall. He nodded, then smiled as he turned his attention back to the fighting demon princes. Asmodeus had explained everything to Edward and ensured his boy would remain in the shadows until the perfect moment.

"Don't forget who controls more legions here than Lucifer, Balam. I can take your minions from under you anytime I choose. I bet you haven't looked at Edward, have you?"

Edward remained standing, but Asmodeus noticed how he shifted into a more dominant pose, feet angled, and knees aligned. His son was ready, waiting for the command to show his strength. Asmodeus smiled at his son's transformation. He was waiting for the right moment to reunite his two sons and see Sully's reaction to Edward's change. As much as Asmodeus longed to keep Edward in a child's form, it was not realistic for Sully's destiny. Transforming Edward was vital to Sully's success, so Asmodeus placed his top demon in charge of the transformation to ensure Edward's success. Looking at Edward, he noted the significant changes in height, body size, and appearance as he grew from child to man. However, he wanted to witness his newfound strength himself rather than hear his demons brag about it. Asmodeus was the demon prince, the strongest of all except Lucifer, but he had always known he would one day succeed Lucifer. This was part of Lucifer's ultimate plan.

Balam changed his tone once Asmodeus pointed out Edward's changes. He could see Balam seething.

"What is this, Asmodeus? Sending THAT child demon back to the hunter to kill us all? See, Astaroth, Beelzebub. Asmodeus feels the need to alter his child's appearance, but he still thinks like a child. Acts like one too. That's where Asmodeus proves he is not capable of being one of us."

Edward clenched his fists, and Asmodeus placed his hand on them to hold him back, to no avail.

"Demon princes, you think of me as a child? Then take me on. I am no longer a child. I can destroy each of you here with no one's help."

Edward flexed his new muscles and cracked his neck. Asmodeus smiled, thinking how similar this was to Sully. That's when he realized Edward had watched and imitated the demon hunter's moves during his time with him. Two different mothers, two different paths—yet each son seemed connected to the other. Former child, now a man. Edward moved with the body dynamics of a muscle-bound athlete and an intelligence so keen and strategic it would only help the hunter protect both Heaven and Hell. Asmodeus had ensured his son's good looks and prowess. Edward wore his dark hair pulled back into a ponytail and his back was covered with demonic tattoos. Why not give his son the gift to attract mortal women above?

Balam shifted but remained silent. He responded with another fist slam on the table. Astaroth hung his head in silence and left the council chambers, leaving Asmodeus and the others staring at Edward. Only Asmodeus smiled. Then Balam left.

***

Despite her fear, Mick tried not to show it. She knew Edward only did what he could to keep them safe, but in her heart, she missed Sully and the earth above. Time was creeping along, and everywhere she and Katarina walked, demons stopped and stared at her. As they walked one path, Mick stopped while Katarina kept going. She was staring right at him—the demon. Her scream drew Katarina back.

"You. I know you. Damn you for what you did to me."

"Little girl, don't you know how I am?" he mocked.

Furious at his tone, Mick closed her eyes and tried to picture her father, Michael—the archangel, one of Heaven's most powerful angels. But she couldn't. Her mind felt fuzzy.

Balam used the moment to grab her and hold her tight. She felt his hand at her temple, and he whispered the exact words he had used when he held her captive. She wasn't going through that again.

"Father, please help me. I don't feel so good."

Before she could utter another word, Mick opened her eyes and found the most beautiful sword she had ever seen in her hands. It was not large, but just the right fit for her. She looked at the blade. An inscription appeared, and she read the words aloud.

"Custos pacis. Guardian of the peace."

Balam looked terrified and dropped his guard. He released her. She used the chance. No longer feeling sick, she urged Katarina to her side. Though they were not best friends yet, Katarina had been comforting her since they arrived. Something unexpected happened—her eyes fluttered, and she almost dropped the sword if not for Katarina's quick hands. She spoke in an unfamiliar voice.

"Remember, I am always with you. Use the sword to strike."

She looked at Balam as he stood before her and closed her eyes. Her arm reached forward, and the sword cut into his side. Breathing hard, she opened her eyes and stared at what she had done. Balam regained his dominance and threw her against the nearest rock. She dropped her sword. She was breathing but could not move. Balam leaned forward and licked her cheek. Mick screamed, and there was silence in response. Then he kissed her.

Mick yelled, "ASMODEUS!"

It was Katarina's voice she heard before she blacked out, followed by the voices of Edward and Asmodeus.

***

Sully was losing his mind without Mick and Katarina. Although he and Elias spent their time researching passages, various ancient texts, and parchments—never knowing where they were—all of this did little to comfort him. He called for his father many times over the last several months, but Asmodeus never came. He felt abandoned. Sully had enough and called for his father one last time. Once again, there was no answer. Before he could react, a stranger appeared.

"Edward, is that you?"

The figure nodded with a sly smile. Sully ran to Edward and embraced him, but then stood back, studying the changes.

"I don't believe it. You're no longer a child! I thought something happened to you with Astaroth and the girls. Where are they?"

Edward's laugh, now deeper, remained the same. "Brother. I'm sorry. I couldn't do what you asked of me while I was a child. I wasn't strong enough, so I asked Asmodeus for help. He devised this plan, and we took Mick and Katarina to Hell."

Edward paused. Sully's eyes changed, and the soul eater emerged. Saliva dripped from his mouth.

"Demon child. Did you take them to Hell? Why do something so foolish? Mick can't go to Hell. My master would devour her in one bite if he got wind of her essence."

Edward gulped, and Sully realized Edward had been gone far too long. "Why isn't father here to help me?"

"It's part of his plan, Sully. He has kept them safe. Especially Mick. He taught her our demon ways, with no one knowing, so she could guide you. Your destiny is just beginning, brother. He wanted me to assist you in strength, cunning, and strategy. I needed a transformation. Astaroth, Balam, and the others are plotting something horrifying for the world. I completed my transformation with one of father's top demons in secret. I can help you now, brother, if you will let me. Father trained me to hone my strength. He asked Mick to teach me man's ways so I don't stand out like what mortals call a freak. Our father took great measures to change me—to aid you as best I can and to teach Mick what she needs to know about demons and Hell."

Sully laughed and embraced his brother harder than the first time. He could hear Elias laughing too, from the back. Relief crossed his face that his brother had returned, though his heart still longed for Mick.

Elias broke the joyous moment with a solemn tone. "Sully, we must address the upcoming uprising targeting you and the world."

This got his attention. Elias stood beside him with a particular book—the book from Asmodeus. Sully took it and urged them all to sit. As he opened it, he felt the book calling to him. He placed the two books side by side. The books trembled, and a blinding light flashed, forcing everyone to shut their eyes. Sully opened them, letting them adjust, and the books had merged into one. He ran his hand over the leather binding, noting how much thicker it had become. The latch caught his eye. It was a lock of some sort. But there was no key required. Extraordinary.

Sully realized his blood held the key to everything he had learned so far. He still didn't understand why. Perhaps his blood was the key to this new book.

"Brother, what happened?"

"Edward, I'm not sure, but I think this was meant to happen."

Elias smiled. "Sully, the book I held is like your father's but greater. It's the companion to that book. It seems it was intended for you. Hopefully you can read the pages in their entirety now that they've merged. I am just your guide. The duty and honor to follow your destiny are yours."

***

Asmodeus knelt, holding Mick's head in his hands. He sought Katarina's explanation but observed her fearful expression. All she could mutter was one word—Balam. His anger rose against his demon brother, but he looked at Mick. He knew how much his son cared for this girl, and his duty was to protect her. Her breathing was shallow but steady.

Katarina regained her composure. "Balam came out of nowhere. He was angry and taunted Mick. Asmodeus, we can't stay here any longer. Mick isn't used to this place. And I miss your son. I think Mick does too. Can we go back to Sully, please?"

Tears flowed down her cheeks. Even for a demon vixen, she had feelings for his son. Something about Sully drew people toward him. Asmodeus couldn't be prouder of his son than he already was, watching the effect he had on Katarina. Though ashamed of using her to keep Sully in Hell, he was still proud.

"Granted. I already sent Edward back to Sully. We must prepare Mick for departure before we can send you both back. I fear she hasn't learned all she needs to, and she can't return to Hell yet, but we must hurry. Come with me. Many tasks, limited time. We must be on guard because what Astaroth and Balam are plotting will destroy everything we worked for. I fear this is the worst to come for my son."

Back in his home, Asmodeus used privacy to his advantage. Letting Mick rest, he ushered Katarina into his entertaining chambers. Despite her constant desire for intimacy, his promise to Sully shifted his focus; keeping the girls safe was more important. He learned a lot about his son through Katarina's memories while she wasn't paying attention. He realized that his son, once a monk, still honored his vows until Mick and Katarina entered his life. As honorable as Sully was, he remained complex and tormented by his birthright. Asmodeus wondered if his acceptance of it would lessen the burden he placed on himself.

"Mick should adapt to the local time and prepare for Balam. I know he entered her mind and took something from her. Despite the barriers, he broke through. That bastard's been gloating about it ever since. I believe it's something about the key and other memories. Powerful memories. You are an unlikely pair of friends, Katarina, but she will need you. I ask you to help her. It's a request, not a command."

Katarina looked at him with simple amazement. "My lord, I will do as you request. I grew to like the girl even if her boyfriend will not father my child."

"Don't be snippy. It's not becoming on you. And her boyfriend is my son. Discover the hidden depth of this pact. It involves me, his mother, Lucifer, and Michael. We aren't easy to kill or fool."

Katarina strutted away, knowing the effect she had on him—Asmodeus had a hard time resisting her—but in the end he did resist. He laughed it off and, since the women were safe in his quarters, decided to respond to his son's unanswered calls. Before leaving, he looked at the recovering woman in his care.

Mick whispered, "Asmodeus. I feel strange. A sword appeared in my hand. I want to go home."

"You will go to my son. He will protect you. However, gain your strength first; I asked Katarina to help prepare you so Balam doesn't hurt you again. Inform Sully upon your return what you have learned thus far. I will return later to check on preparations and get you women back to him. You can't stay here anymore, and Edward is with Sully now."

2

While Abaddon observed, the hunter and the prophet stayed inside the apartment building. Astaroth wanted the prophet, but she could not harm him, which complicated things with the hunter. However, Astaroth sent his demons to accompany her with instructions to capture Elias. While they entered the building, she remained outside and waited. Once they captured the prophet, she was to search for the key. She saw a flash of light emanating from the hunter's apartment.

What the fuck was that? As the intense light faded into darkness once more, she waited to make her move. Figures moved around the room, and she was growing impatient. Before she turned around, Astaroth was beside her.

"Tell me what you see. Where's the prophet?"

"Inside. I know Balam failed you last time, but I won't. I will give you the prophet, but the hunter and I have unfinished business first."

"Leave him alone. I was clear. I don't need him interfering now. Play with your toy later. Asmodeus has something up his sleeve, and I need that prophet and his secrets." He disappeared as quickly as he came.

While the blue sky faded, Abaddon observed the darkness closing in. She, a night demon, favored attacking in darkness. She called for a few lesser demons to distract the hunter while the others captured the prophet. She sent two waves of Astaroth's demons to do the dirty work. She watched one demon—he was too fidgety and in need of flexing his muscles. Men, she thought.

Grabbing his hand, she led him to a secluded spot and threw him onto the tiniest bit of grass she could find. Straddling him, she lunged forward into a kiss. Since he was a lesser demon, he had to serve her. She ran her hands up and down his torso, undoing his belt. Abaddon was in heat before he could even undress her. She allowed him to remove her clothes as she tore at his. His mouth nibbled at her breasts while she caressed him with fervor. She stared at his body, drooling over his tight abs. Moving her tongue down his torso, she kept her eyes on him. One thing about her sexual appetite was that she always had to look into her partner's eyes to ensure her dominance. He looked into her eyes and moaned as she massaged his manhood. His hands grasped her hips as he pushed her down on him, and she let him slide into her. At the height of pleasure, she let out a satisfied yet quiet scream.

"When I summon you, you must come to me."

"Yes. Yes, Abaddon. I will obey your command."

"Good. Now get dressed. I'm done with you for now. We need to get the prophet."

Abaddon followed the demons into the apartment building, and they prepared to make their move against the hunter.

***

With a pricked finger, Sully released a small drop of blood into the lock. The lock loosened, and the book opened to one of many pages. Blank at first, it changed when his hand contacted the paper. That's when he read to the others:

The child becomes the man, who then protects both darkness and light. In the darkness, the hounds wait for those who serve the light. The hounds from hell will seek the blood of the protector. The protector must guard the darkness to keep the path closed.

Perplexed by what he had just read, Sully paused. Since his finger was still bleeding, he touched the page again. His blood mixed with the words, and the page changed. He continued reading:

The skies will blacken as the sun fades. The prophet's voice will cease when the fallen take him. The protector needs to choose—his mortal enemies or his oath.

When Sully completed the passage, dread washed over him as he glanced toward Elias and Edward. Edward's new appearance fascinated him. As he pondered, he contemplated Edward's potential against demons. Elias broke the silence.

"Sully, that was the most unusual text we've come across. Of course, the last part you read talks about me. I'm the only prophet standing at your side, and I don't like it."

"Elias, you're right. Edward, what do you think?"

Edward swallowed hard and didn't answer. Before Sully could place why, demons burst through the door. *Great, here we go again.* Sully grabbed his sword, readying himself, until Abaddon came into view.

"Hunter."

"Bitch."

After he realized her part in attacking Mick, he admitted his attitude toward her had changed. He was no longer the fool for this demon. With his sword held steady and his feet spread, he prepared for her attack. She didn't move. Sully cursed but remained silent and still. He whispered to the Soul Eater:

"I'll lead the way, and you can savor the demons' defeat."

Sully could feel the Soul Eater's excitement. Ever since they agreed to the alliance, and since he accepted his birthright, Sully had become stronger and more bloodthirsty.

Abaddon sneered. "The little demon is now a man. Isn't that precious?"

Edward glanced at Sully and nodded. Armed with his sword, Sully was prepared for anything. Looking left, he caught sight of Elias brandishing his fighting staff. During their months of isolation, Sully had prepared Elias to battle demons, but they had encountered none until now.

The demons advanced toward Sully and Edward. Abaddon didn't move. The first demon approached Edward, snarling with fists up. After centuries of having Edward at his side, Sully was ready to protect him—until he saw Edward hurl the demon against the wall with one hand. It wasn't a regular fighting move but something impressive. Sully realized his brother could fight for himself and alongside him. His father had seen to that.

Sully played his usual games with the demons, recognizing the hunger from the Soul Eater. In recent months, the Soul Eater and Sully had grown closer and embraced their alliance. The Soul Eater was becoming a confidant, but Sully didn't want it getting arrogant. He stared down the other demons in the room as the Soul Eater stirred. They feared him—or they feared the sword in his hand. It didn't matter. That's when he saw Abaddon move closer to Elias. Elias was afraid. Something was amiss.

Elias assumed the fundamental fighting stance Sully had taught him. Sully smiled at the man's progress. Even though Elias raised and readied his staff, Sully knew he was no match for the demon bitch. Before Sully could move toward Elias, Asmodeus appeared out of nowhere.

"Abaddon! What in Lucifer's name are you up to?"

"Asmodeus. We're just having a little fun, weren't we, hunter?"

Unhappy about not getting his taste of blood, the Soul Eater spoke through Sully. Feeling the hunger for a fight, Sully grabbed one demon and clamped him in a tight chokehold, the demon's hands beating against Sully's forearms. Though he didn't need to use his sword, he said, "Submittere."

The demon said, "Parere dominus."

Abaddon screamed when she heard the words from the demon. Asmodeus flicked his finger and sent her back to Hell. The other demons scrambled to escape the apartment, leaving their friend in Sully's arms.

"Dammit, Father. I wanted to know her intentions. Someone sent her here—we've had months of peace since the desert."

"Sit down, Sully. Let me fill you in on all the shit that's broken loose in Hell."

***

Mick regained her strength and saw that Katarina was watching over her. She struggled a little to sit up but managed the task.

"Good, you're up. Asmodeus will send us back to Sully after you regain strength and prepare yourself. Upon our return, things may appear different. But he wants me to make sure you are strong and healed. We're unsure about your situation, but we're returning to Sully and the rest."

Mick felt elated upon hearing the news, but her mind was foggy and disoriented. She figured she had been in Hell too long, though she was no expert.

"I'm glad. Katarina, can I ask you a favor? Did you get my sword that appeared in my hands before?"

"Yes. I put it away to keep it safe from the demons. Asmodeus saw and knew, yet remained silent. He claimed secrecy for safety, but it should accompany us above. Let me get it."

Mick took the sword and glanced at Katarina. She didn't get to say a word before demons broke into Asmodeus' home. Katarina motioned for silence, and both women snuck away. Still feeling weak, Mick heard the voice inside her once more.

"Trust me, Michael's daughter. I am Cassiel. Use the sword when needed, but leave Hell with the demon Katarina now. Follow the path past the darkest part of Hell, and you will see the stairs. Take the stairs and head up. Michael is protecting you. The stairs will only appear to you, so you must guide the demon. You are the beacon. Both of you are required for what lies ahead. The hunter needs you."

While she listened, the demons destroyed everything in the front room. She knew they would come for them. Mick took the lead and guided Katarina out of Asmodeus' home. Seeing a dark path illuminate, she whispered, "Do you see it?"

Katarina replied, "See what?"

"Never mind. Just follow me. I guess it's only something I can see because of who my father is. Take my hand."

Mick heard the demons following. They must have picked up their scent. With her sword in one hand and the other feeling along the walls, she led Katarina through the darkest parts of Hell, moving faster. Her racing heart yearned for Sully, yet she questioned the dynamics of this love triangle. Sully had promised to sleep with Katarina—but at his choosing—while he was interested in her. Mick knew Sully had made this bargain for her help, but she found it awkward since Katarina was becoming her friend.

Still guiding Katarina, Mick followed the angel's instructions. Two demons appeared behind them just before they reached the darkest part of Hell. There was no time to react, because Katarina screamed and started tugging on Mick. Mick faced Balam again. She screamed. The demons held Katarina while Balam caressed her cheek. Before she knew it, his tongue slid up her cheek as he breathed on her. Mick was about to knee him in the groin but stopped when he pulled away.

He sniffed the air and came closer to her face to smell her. While Balam looked confused, Mick gripped her sword and struck him with it. Balam staggered, clutching his side and balling his fist. She wasn't sure if he would strike her in retaliation, but she would not give him the chance. Mick pointed her sword at him, gripping it with two hands while she set her legs in a fighting stance. She noticed Katarina could not help her. Mick took a deep breath and whispered, "Father, help me if you can."

As she readied herself, Balam faltered—but not much. He still held tight to his side, his demon blood gushing out. Seeing the injury, her confidence grew.

"Do you want another taste of me, demon? I am no longer afraid of your kind."

She hoped he wouldn't call her bluff. Instead, he snickered.

"I have what I need. I don't need you, plaything. I want Katarina."

Mick saw fear and confusion in Katarina's eyes. Remaining steadfast, she waited. When no one moved, she strode forward and lunged her sword at Balam. This time, he was ready and moved the other way. Her feet pivoted, she swung the blade in a wide circle, and lunged—this time cutting into Balam's other side.

"Tell your demons to let her go, or my next strike will be like Sully's attacks. Who do you think taught me to use a sword, demon?"

Balam relented and spoke to the demons. "Let her go. We'll return for her later."

The demons left the women and followed Balam toward another opening in Hell. Fearful, Mick had to escape. As she and Katarina made their way through the darkest part of their journey, she slipped against the rock.

"Ouch!"

Katarina rushed to her side and tried to help her. Grateful, Mick knew she couldn't do this alone. As they continued, she noticed Katarina kept looking back, as if expecting something—or someone—to appear. Snarls emerged from the tunnels. Mick's heart raced as she pulled Katarina, urging her to keep moving forward—faster.

Asmodeus' home. Katarina motioned for silence, and both women snuck away. Still feeling weak, Mick heard the voice inside her once more.

"Trust me, Michael's daughter. I am Cassiel. Use the sword when needed, but leave Hell with the demon Katarina now. Follow the path past the darkest part of Hell, and you will see the stairs. Take the stairs and head up. Michael is protecting you. The stairs will only appear to you, so you must guide the demon. You are the beacon. Both of you are required for what lies ahead. The hunter needs you."

While she listened, the demons destroyed everything in the front room. She knew they would come for them. Mick took the lead and guided Katarina out of Asmodeus' home. Seeing a dark path illuminate, she whispered, "Do you see it?"

Katarina replied, "See what?"

"Never mind. Just follow me. I guess it's only something I can see because of who my father is. Take my hand."

Mick heard the demons following. They must have picked up their scent. With her sword in one hand and the other feeling along the walls, she led Katarina through the darkest parts of Hell, moving faster. Her racing heart yearned for Sully, yet she questioned the dynamics of this love triangle. Sully had promised to sleep with Katarina—but at his choosing—while he was interested in her. Mick knew Sully had made this bargain for her help, but she found it awkward since Katarina was becoming her friend.

Still guiding Katarina, Mick followed the angel's instructions. Two demons appeared behind them just before they reached the darkest part of Hell. There was no time to react, because Katarina screamed and started tugging on Mick. Mick faced Balam again. She screamed. The demons held Katarina while Balam caressed her cheek. Before she knew it, his tongue slid up her cheek as he breathed on her. Mick was about to knee him in the groin but stopped when he pulled away.

He sniffed the air and came closer to her face to smell her. While Balam looked confused, Mick gripped her sword and struck him with it. Balam staggered, clutching his side and balling his fist. She wasn't sure if he would strike her in retaliation, but she would not give him the chance. Mick pointed her sword at him, gripping it with two hands while she set her legs in a fighting stance. She noticed Katarina could not help her. Mick took a deep breath and whispered, "Father, help me if you can."

As she readied herself, Balam faltered—but not much. He still held tight to his side, his demon blood gushing out. Seeing the injury, her confidence grew.

"Do you want another taste of me, demon? I am no longer afraid of your kind."

She hoped he wouldn't call her bluff. Instead, he snickered.

"I have what I need. I don't need you, plaything. I want Katarina."

Mick saw fear and confusion in Katarina's eyes. Remaining steadfast, she waited. When no one moved, she strode forward and lunged her sword at Balam. This time, he was ready and moved the other way. Her feet pivoted, she swung the blade in a wide circle, and lunged—this time cutting into Balam's other side.

"Tell your demons to let her go, or my next strike will be like Sully's attacks. Who do you think taught me to use a sword, demon?"

Balam relented and spoke to the demons. "Let her go. We'll return for her later."

The demons left the women and followed Balam toward another opening in Hell. Fearful, Mick had to escape. As she and Katarina made their way through the darkest part of their journey, she slipped against the rock.

"Ouch!"

Katarina rushed to her side and tried to help her. Grateful, Mick knew she couldn't do this alone. As they continued, she noticed Katarina kept looking back, as if expecting something—or someone—to appear. Snarls emerged from the tunnels. Mick's heart raced as she pulled Katarina, urging her to keep moving forward—faster.

3

Asmodeus motioned for Edward, Sully, and Elias to take a seat. He walked around, searching for something. Rummaging through the scattered papers on the table, he found the merged book. As his fingers touched the cover, the book opened to him. Asmodeus noticed the strange looks he was getting from Sully and Elias.

"A lot has happened in Hell while you roamed the earth, my son. Do you still possess the key? Show me."

Sully took the key from his pants pocket and held it up for him to see. Asmodeus smiled and looked at Edward. He observed Edward edging toward the door, ear pressed against it. Asmodeus continued.

"The demon princes are after that key. First, you found Mick in Los Angeles, the premier demon-hunting city in California. Next, your team journeys to the First Garden, an exclusive place of serenity for the worthy. Now, my son, you are in a new city, searching books for what? Do you have a clear idea of what you're seeking?"

Asmodeus paused, realizing he had raised his voice and hadn't meant to. Knowing the limited time he had, he understood the women's need to return to Sully. Asmodeus lifted his nose to the air and sniffed. One hand smoothed his long black hair while the other reached for the sword strapped across his back. Acknowledging Edward, he nodded while gripping the handle, preparing for what awaited beyond. He looked at his son and said, "Soul Eater, I command you to obey me as you obey Lucifer."

Sully stood in obedience, and his eyes shifted from their deep blue to blue and yellow. Asmodeus could feel the Soul Eater's presence, and Elias sat in disbelief, unaware of what was happening. Asmodeus commanded the room with his voice.

"Soul Eater, protect the prophet at all costs. With what lies ahead, you must be in control of my son to safeguard his fate. I command you as Lucifer's Successor and High Prince Demon. What say you, Soul Eater?"

The Soul Eater's voice came from Sully's lips. "I am here to serve. I only ask for the blood of demons to fill my appetite."

"Granted. Now protect the prophet."

Asmodeus turned to Edward. "Edward, it's your turn to shine, my boy. Show those rogues your new power. I waited to see the outcome of the transformation. Make me proud and show me your true nature."

Edward smiled. Asmodeus couldn't be prouder of his two favorite sons. As he readied himself, Asmodeus sent a silent message to Edward. His transformation included telepathic abilities to assist Sully in times like this.

A panic-stricken look appeared in Elias's eyes—Asmodeus saw it. He nodded to Sully, and the Soul Eater took complete control of his son. Sully began chanting in the ancient demonic language. The door flew off its hinges, and both Astaroth and Balam stood in the frame with at least ten demons behind them. Edward faced the two demons and, as he raised his hand, a flash of lightning emerged from his fingers; he aimed it straight into Astaroth's chest. Balam moved to strike.

Balam lunged past Edward and went straight for Elias. Asmodeus said only one word. "Soul Eater."

Sully stepped before Elias and raised his sword. His movements were quick and skilled as he brought the blade down in a circular motion and released his grip. The sword struck Balam in the chest as his body slid to the ground; Sully's foot sideswiped the demon so he fell on his back. With the sword back in his grip, Sully slid his finger down its long blade and tasted the demon's blood. Asmodeus saw a hunger in his son's eyes that would make any demon cringe in fear, and he understood why Lucifer favored his most treasured servant. Sully reached his hand into the demon's chest and fed on his blood and life. He looked at the next demon, licking his lips and salivating, while Asmodeus watched with a hint of disgust.

"Look at the little pet. Do you want to play with the Soul Eater, demon?"

Sully taunted the demons and licked his lips with more hunger as he pointed the sword's tip at them. Asmodeus watched his sons in action, pleased with what he had created. Then he saw Sully raise his free hand and, with a quick curl of his finger, one demon slid across the way into his grip. Sully brought the demon's head close to his lips with one hand and bit the demon's ear, letting blood trickle into his mouth. Without dropping his sword, Sully drank while the others watched in fear. As he reached for the next demon, Asmodeus couldn't watch any longer. With a flick of his hand, he sent the demons back to Hell, leaving Sully still holding one lifeless demon.

Astaroth hunched over in pain, and when Asmodeus turned his attention toward him, he saw Edward standing over him and driving an elbow into his back. As Astaroth fell, Balam summoned more demons into the apartment. Soon, Sully faced attacks from all sides while the prophet did his best to fight them off. Edward was quick and killed several demons with his powerful hands, while Asmodeus moved toward a crippled Astaroth. He bent down, grabbed him by the hair, and lifted his face so Astaroth could stare into his eyes.

"As you were saying in Hell, brother? You were going to destroy my son?"

Astaroth spit at Asmodeus and laughed.

"Oh, brother, you are the fool. This was not a full-blown attack. It was a mere distraction after you revealed your true intentions at the council meeting. We needed to learn your alliances and which side you will stand on when we enter the kingdom of Heaven."

As Asmodeus surveyed the room, he spotted the demons encircling Sully and the prophet; in fact, the demons appeared to be winning against Sully—until he changed the situation. Despite being hurt, Balam still faced Sully, while Astaroth, panting, showed no signs of surrender. With gritted teeth, Asmodeus reached for Astaroth's throat. As his hands closed around his neck, he seethed and growled.

"Brother, my alliances are not your concern. All I care about is serving Lucifer. The pact kept our kingdom safe, but you feel the need to break it. Why? Are you not afraid of the destruction that awaits us if you break the pact?"

"Damn, you are a bigger fool than we thought. Lucifer is no longer interested in the pact. Balam will use the women to convince you once he controls your son's little girlfriend. You're too focused on the pact and the demon hunter to remember how much you wanted into Heaven to destroy the angels. Think, Asmodeus, think. Imagine your power becoming so much like Lucifer's that all of Hell would rule this forsaken land. It's what you wanted. You just need to remember, brother."

Asmodeus had heard enough. He clapped his hands together and commanded Astaroth and Balam, along with the remaining demons, to return to Hell. The room flashed, and the floor opened, revealing a pit of fire. However, this was not his doing. Asmodeus trembled in secret. Lucifer's face appeared through the flames as a long red arm reached for Astaroth and yanked him back into the fiery pits of Hell. Lucifer's lips curved into a wicked smile that sent Asmodeus a single message only he would understand. After Sully's battle for the key, Asmodeus had spoken to Lucifer, requesting permission to safeguard the women and locate the rebel demons plotting against him. It was their secret to protect. All was going according to plan.

4

Balam and Astaroth sat in the throne room in silence as Lucifer watched them with consternation from his throne. The two demons paced back and forth in fear while Beelzebub looked on with amusement. It was Astaroth who finally broke the silence with a snide remark.

"Lucifer, we all know you favor Asmodeus, but you must break the pact you agreed to eons ago. We are the trinity of Hell. The demon hunter claimed his birthright and received your blessing. We agreed the pact must end once he claimed it—and he did. We must prepare for the battle."

Lucifer sat, rubbing his chin with his right hand. He sought words to appease the others while secretly contemplating his next move.

"I hear you, but the trinity is you, me, and Beelzebub. Not Balam—though he comes in handy with the hunter and the woman. Where is the woman under Asmodeus' protection?"

Balam said, "She's in the caverns of the darkest part. She's trying to escape, but I heard your hellhounds were in the caves, watching her and Katarina. I don't think they'll get far or return to Asmodeus' home. What do you want with the hunter's girlfriend? What's so special about her?"

Fuming at Balam's remark, Lucifer sent the demon away with a single glance—banishing him to another cave. Hell filled with Balam's screams, delivering a simple message to all servants and lesser demons: Lucifer would not tolerate failure. He had long wanted to send Balam to the screaming souls room—his personal playground—for his repeated failures to destroy the hunter. Every time he had tried, Astaroth had interfered. But not this time. Lucifer relished his amusement as he turned his gaze on Astaroth, who now stood subdued in fear.

"No one is to touch the woman or Katarina. The hounds will not seek her out. We are the trinity, but don't forget that Hell is my kingdom, and you serve me."

Beelzebub nodded silently in agreement. Once again, Lucifer asserted his dominion. Without a word, he summoned his hounds. Soon, they were at his feet, all three glaring at Astaroth and Beelzebub, awaiting their master's command. With his left hand, he stroked their heads in praise, pride gleaming in his eyes. Among all his hellhounds, these three were his most prized.

He had named the middle hound Raphael—as a reminder of his arch-enemy. The last, he named Eve, for the satisfaction it brought him. She was formidable, the mother of many hellhounds, and her namesake delighted him: the one child of his Father so easily turned. Cerberus, the leader of the trio, was the most feared of all. He had mated Eve and Cerberus countless times to build his army. He controlled them—except on rare occasions when he commanded them to obey another.

Lucifer rose from the throne and motioned for Astaroth and Beelzebub to follow. The hounds remained steadfast and alert.

"Bring me the woman. No hellhound will harm her... yet."

The two demons departed in search of the hunter's girlfriend.

***

Mick continued to run along the walls of Hell in search of the stairs, but none appeared. She urged Katarina to follow, but panic set in when she heard heavy footsteps echoing from a tunnel.

"Katarina, we need to go back to Asmodeus' home. No stairs in sight, no way out."

Katarina pulled her toward another passage, and they ran until they reached Asmodeus's dwelling. Mick clutched her sword tightly, but before they could reach the door, two demons blocked their path. She recognized Astaroth but said nothing. Tightening her grip, she stood defiant, ready for their attack.

Astaroth laughed. "Foolish woman. You can't win against any of us in Hell. With Asmodeus gone, no one is here to protect you. But Katarina—she may be fun to toy with."

Beelzebub lunged at Mick and grabbed her sword. Unarmed, she panicked but refused to show fear. His hand brushed her cheek, reminding her of Balam's disgusting touch. Thinking of Sully, she kicked Beelzebub in the groin. As the demon hunched over, Astaroth laughed again.

Mick saw Astaroth raise his hand and mime strangling her. Her breath caught, and she struggled for air. Desperate, her eyes searched for Katarina—only to find her unconscious on the ground. Mick knew she couldn't leave Hell without her and surrendered. Beelzebub scooped Katarina's limp body into his arms and walked away. Astaroth relaxed his grip, and Mick collapsed, gasping for breath.

Still, she refused to relinquish her sword. Her determination caught Astaroth's attention.

"Be still, woman. Keep your precious sword for now. Lucifer only wants a word with you. You will face the King of Hell. You should feel honored."

He snickered, mocking her.

"Fuck you, demon."

"Don't resist. Just follow me—or I'll feed you to the hounds."

Mick followed Astaroth, and while walking, she paid close attention to the way they traveled. She noticed Astaroth's stride was a bit off compared to before. Upon seeing his injuries, she realized they were recent. With a thought, she smiled. *Astaroth must've* been in a fight with *either* Sully or Asmodeus. *There was still* hope!

She ran her fingers through her short, dark hair and breathed as her mind pondered about the different ways her conversation with Lucifer could go. She was going to meet the damn devil himself and sensed her fears growing. A voice echoed in her mind and became louder.

"Daughter, you are not alone. Remain steadfast, and we'll uncover a way out of Hell for you. Your destiny is not done."

Mick smiled faintly, though it vanished once they entered the throne room. The sight before her drained the color from her face. The chamber was vast and terrible in its grandeur. On the throne sat Lucifer himself.

She trembled at his presence—dark hair, high cheekbones, a perfect nose, and eyes as black as the night sky. Clad in a black suit, he exuded regality and power. His beauty captivated her even as terror gripped her. At his feet sat three enormous hounds. At first they looked like three separate beasts, but when she blinked, she realized they shared one body.

Lucifer noticed her staring and rose from the throne.

"Are you admiring my beautiful hounds, woman?"

Mick coughed, regaining composure. "They are large. But I see three heads on one body. That's not normal, is it?"

The handsome man laughed. "They share one body when protecting me. They separate at my command—or their own will. You carry a power-ful weapon, but I do not fear you. Sheath your sword, and they will know you mean me no harm."

Mick hesitated, then sheathed her blade. With a wave of his hand, the hound shifted—splitting from one body into three. Lucifer stepped closer until he stood before her, though still at a safe distance. Extending his hand, he waited for her to take it.

"Come with me, woman. We need to talk. Just you and me."

Mick steadied her courage. "Call me Mick, not woman. I am not yours to command. How do you know who I am?"

Lucifer inhaled the air around her, then reached out and gently tugged at her hair, breathing in her scent. Pulling back, he turned toward the doorway.

"Ah. So my brother, the archangel, is a father! That makes you my niece, Mick. Does the hunter know what you are? Does he know what you possess?"

He sneered. Mick's chest tightened. Why did he want to talk to her? He was Lucifer—her uncle. The thought chilled her. She placed her sword on the floor, trembling at her own boldness.

Am I fucked now?

"What do you want, Lucifer? I may be trapped here, but I have Asmodeus' protection. Even your thugs know that."

"Let's talk, my niece."

Lucifer motioned for her to follow, his three hounds padding at his side.

"These are my hellhounds. They will not harm you as I have commanded—unless you raise that sword against me. Carry it or leave it. Your choice. Beelzebub, Astaroth—dismissed. You heard me call her my niece. You will not harm her... not unless I say so. Place Katarina in Asmodeus' home. Do not touch her. He granted her protection, and I will honor it. I will not risk war in my kingdom."

Beelzebub and Astaroth left. Alone now, Mick's fear deepened. Lucifer was far more terrifying than any thug she had ever faced in her mortal life.

5

Once Sully regained control and the apartment was cleansed of the demons' attack, he let his temper loose on everyone around him—including his trusted friend and prophet, Elias. After drinking the demons' blood, the Soul Eater was quiet and satiated. Sully, however, was in no mood for the bullshit coming from his father's lips. He grabbed the book in front of him and hurled it against the wall, then felt Edward's hand on him.

"Brother, you can't lose your temper. Listen to Father as he tells you what has happened in Hell while you sat here with the prophet. You need to listen, or you will lose the women. This time, the demons are serious. You have what they want—the key."

Sully slammed his fist into the wall, leaving a hole. He glanced at Elias and lowered his eyes in shame. Elias stepped closer to console him, and Sully felt something rare: a sense of being lost.

"I'm sorry. I will listen, Father. Speak truth, answer me, or witness kingdoms crumble. This is my promise to both you and my mother."

As he made the promise, he felt the Soul Eater stirring within. Sully, yearning to provide sustenance, sensed its hunger. The thought of drinking demons' blood sickened him, yet he couldn't deny the craving. For months, the Soul Eater had fed only when needed, but the taste of demon blood was more satisfying. Little by little, Sully felt himself slipping deeper into the pact. He had accepted his birthright, but since that moment, he had lost the two women who meant the most to him. He was left with only Elias, and his mother, Jophiel, had gone silent. He felt abandoned. Too much had been placed on him. Looking at Asmodeus, he nodded. He was ready to hear the truth.

Asmodeus sighed and began.

"Before you lose your damn temper again—the women are safe. Katarina is ideal for Mick's protection, but I don't know for how long. I'm trying to get them back to you. My son, listen. Edward is prepared to stand beside you as an adult, not a child. Elias... well, I must leave that to your mother and Michael. Once you claimed your birthright and both kingdoms merged their weapons to give you that sword, you set something in motion no one expected. Legions of demons rejected serving Lucifer or the pact. That's where Astaroth, Balam, and Beelzebub come in. They desire something, but I'm uncertain of its nature. Lucifer wants something. Everyone in Hell wants something—because you found the key and took it from its sacred hiding place. I don't know if the key was ever meant to leave. I don't know what's coming. All I know, my son, is that I promised your mother I would protect you and serve you without question. But even now, I wonder—what is your plan?"

"My plan? Damnit, I don't know what my plan is. I swore to protect the pact with every fiber of my soul, but that was before I lost Mick and Katarina. The answer must be here somewhere. Edward, brother, help me and Elias find it. Asmodeus, Father—don't speak in riddles. Is Hell in chaos, or must I descend to see for myself?"

He slammed his fist once more into the wall. Elias shrugged in despair and confusion.

"Why did they want the prophet? What do they want from him?"

Asmodeus sighed again, glancing at him. Sully knew he was holding something back. This wasn't just about demons disliking the pact. They wanted the prophet, they wanted him, they wanted Mick and Katarina. Why?

He reached for his sword, waiting for Asmodeus to answer.

The demon lowered his head, his voice quiet.

"Deciding between sides will trigger war—resulting in humanity's destruction and chaos, with uncertain consequences. Choosing Hell binds you to Lucifer as his personal hunter, enslaving the world you knew. The pact doesn't mention it, but some believe the hunter's allegiance will shift to Lucifer. People will lose their free will. Demons will leave Hell's gates open to the world. Lucifer's dominion will grow. No balance means Heaven will fall. No gates to protect either side.

"And then, the other possibility—you choose Heaven, and Lucifer's grasp tightens on those already in Hell. He'll unleash the hounds to kill those who resist, and he'll use your mother and Mick's father as his toys. I know Mick's uniqueness. I've kept it secret from the other demons. You must stay the course and honor the destiny you accepted. Find the key's purpose. Guard it."

Sully dropped his sword and looked at Elias, then at Asmodeus. Emotion rarely surfaced in him—except when it concerned his mother. In the short time he had known her, he had been fiercely protective. The Soul Eater felt his pain and spoke to him.

Trust your father, hunter. You and I are one. I cannot let anyone harm you, and you cannot harm me. Our alliance is strong, but we may need permanent unity. We must merge instead of you calling me only when needed. Our bond must strengthen.

Sully paced, furious, contemplating his father's words. He picked up his sword and stormed out of the apartment. At that moment, he disregarded everyone else's thoughts. He knew only that he had to find Mick and Katarina. He felt torn between them. One he had promised to bed—though he lacked experience with women—while the other felt perfect. His heart was split between them.

He walked for several minutes before reaching a dark alley. Pointing his sword downward in reverence to Hell, he recalled the words from the book. Speaking the words aloud, a portal opened in the ground. He wondered if rescuing the women was a mistake. Did it mean favoring one side? He didn't know anymore.

As Asmodeus's words echoed in his mind, he closed the portal and returned to the apartment. He was the demon hunter, yet inside he felt broken. But then, a demon caught his attention. Sully readied his sword. He lacked patience to parley; he preferred killing demons. He missed the days of hunting without caring about the pact. Raising his blade, he felt a nagging in his subconscious. The demon danced around him. Sully didn't move.

"Do you want to dance with me, little demon?"

The demon smiled and shifted—child, man, woman. Sully's patience frayed. Before he could strike, his mother's voice echoed in his mind.

"*The oath, my son. Remember the oath you took. Maintain the balance, or everything—including your soul—will be lost.*"

The demon kept circling, teasing him to strike. Sully sheathed his sword and steadied himself. If he needed to fight, he would with fists, not steel. The demon lunged, and Sully shifted. He caught her arm, twisted, and slammed her onto her back. In one motion, he straddled her and pinned her arms. She writhed beneath him, then spoke.

"Hunter, I bring you an invitation to Hell. Choose to stay with us in Hell."

"Sounds tempting, demon. Who's summoning?"

The demon laughed. "Abaddon wants you to join her. You could rule your own league of demons."

"Tell your demon leader bitch that if she wants me, she can come find me. I'll only visit Hell to see my father. Nothing more. A visit—not to join Abaddon, Astaroth, Beelzebub, or any of those other dimwitted assholes."

Sully wrestled her until the Soul Eater woke within. His eyes shifted—one blue, one yellow—and the demon stared in horror.

"Oh, little demon. Remember me?"

She gulped. "Soul Eater... I would not harm the hunter. I only had orders. You know what happens when Abaddon is disobeyed."

Laughter erupted.

"Little, pathetic demon. You don't understand. I serve one master—Lucifer. But the hunter and I have an agreement. I use him to drink demon blood to sate my thirst, especially from those already doomed. Leave, or the hunter destroys you and I consume your blood. This won't affect his choices. Your master broke the rules. Go back. Tell Abaddon I await her pleasure—but the hunter will not join her. Fail, and I'll drink every drop from you."

The demon bowed her head in submission. The Soul Eater withdrew and slumbered once more.

"Hunter, we will meet again. My master will have you on your knees at her side like a dog."

She fled before Sully could destroy her and drink her blood.

6

Abaddon faced the demon who returned without Sully. Even as she listened to the demon's story, she was furious.

"Abaddon, you aren't listening. The Soul Eater is within the hunter—it's like they are one or something. Did Lucifer send him to help the hunter? The hunter feeds on our blood now, or at least the Soul Eater does. It's confusing how they are one, but the hunter won't come. What do you require of me now, mistress?"

While she listened, the idea of the hunter and the Soul Eater together grew more tempting, urging her to see it herself. She needed a way to the hunter. As she sat in silence, Astaroth and Beelzebub interrupted her thoughts. Behind them followed Balam.

Her glare fell upon Balam, the weaker of the three.

"Come here, Balam. Face me."

Balam stood before her, and before he could speak, Abaddon raised her right hand and slapped him across the cheek.

"Damn fools. You can't catch two women—especially one who doesn't know her way around Hell—and you can't capture the prophet. What good are you to me, you idiots?"

Astaroth and Beelzebub remained steadfast, but Balam took the brunt of her wrath.

"Mistress, the hunter was there, and Asmodeus fought with them."

Abaddon glared, then faced the other two demons. Her face reddened; as she seethed, her hands clenched and she hurled fireballs at them. Her hair fell around her face and her eyes burned. She noticed Astaroth flinch, but he said nothing.

"You asked me for help and yet you stand in silence. What is it you are after, Astaroth?"

Astaroth moved closer and leaned toward her. He whispered,

"I will replace Lucifer and rule this kingdom. Hell will bow before me, and I will end the foolish pact that kept me from my trophy. Hell needs change. I will claim the hunter as my most prized possession. And what I have in store for you, sweet Abaddon, will please you. You are one of Lucifer's chosen. I can choose you to be my champion—the champion who will destroy the world."

Smiling, Abaddon stepped back. With her right foot forward, she settled her weight. Licking her lips in delight, she smiled at Astaroth. With her right hand, she reached behind her for her blade. Before she could strike, Astaroth had already grabbed her wrist midair. She kept her smile as she glared into his eyes. Without hesitation, her left hand blasted fire into his side. The scent of burned flesh rose as he clutched his wound.

"Bitch!"

"You want my help, yet you keep the hunter for yourself? And what of Katarina and the woman? Are they to be yours too? Seems unfair to me when I am more powerful than you. Remember, Astaroth, I can do what you cannot."

Reeling from pain, he let her move closer. She whispered in his ear, "I will keep the hunter, the woman, and Katarina. In exchange, Lucifer's downfall will be your victory alone. I will deliver him to you—and the heads of his hellhounds on a silver platter. You claim victory, and the hunter will be my new plaything. If I get my desires, you can enslave Asmodeus and any demon. Deal?"

Astaroth nodded and walked away, the other demons following behind.

***

Mick was in disbelief as she glanced around the adorned room Lucifer had brought her to. Candles provided the only light in the dim space. The couch looked comfortable and inviting, but she dared not sit—at least not yet. She wasn't about to give her "uncle" the satisfaction of thinking she had accepted anything after learning she was Michael's daughter. Lucifer poured drinks while his hounds sat near her, watching her every move.

He handed her a glass and sat, staring. Mick shifted and broke the silence.

"I want to go home. Asmodeus was going to help me leave this place. Let me go home."

Lucifer sneered. "Let me go home, what?"

Mick bit her lip. "Let me go home, please."

Lucifer smiled. "Can't call me uncle? You're related to me, after all. My brother, Michael the archangel, had a daughter. We'll skip that part for now, niece. *Niece*... has a nice ring to it, don't you think?"

Mick grew impatient. Lucifer must have noticed, because he shifted farther from her but ordered his hounds to sleep. She was furious at herself for falling into this damn trap. Still, there might be a way to extract information from her "uncle."

"Okay, Lucifer. I'll play the uncle–niece game and see where it gets me. I've lived on L.A. streets; Hell can't be that different. What's your purpose regarding Sully?"

Lucifer adjusted his black shirt and leaned back on the couch. With a snap, a gorgeous woman appeared, carrying food. Mick's patience thinned. "What do you want with Sully? With me?"

Lucifer set aside his drink and waved the woman away. He smiled at Mick—then the smile vanished. Mick tensed but waited, refusing to let him see her fear. Her fate, she realized, was in her uncle's hands. Still, Lucifer said nothing. His gaze was solemn.

"You've asked me several times what I want. It's simple. I want the hunter—the son of Asmodeus. If the rumors are true, he and the Soul Eater are one. The Soul Eater is my servant, which makes the hunter mine. And if I believe my demons, he has the key. I want it all. The sweetest part, my niece, is that I want *you* to bring it all to me. Then you can return to your home and your life. I'll leave you alone—or we can enjoy your visits to Hell. Doesn't matter to me, niece."

Mick swallowed hard. Inside, she was crying. Her life in exchange for Sully serving Lucifer—it didn't seem right. She longed to reconnect with Sully, but not at that cost. She resolved to defy him and find another way. "No."

Lucifer's face contorted, anger flashing. She felt the hatred in his stare. As she shifted in her seat, he called to his hounds.

"Watch her. If she so much as moves a muscle, kill her. If she grabs her sword, kill her. I will return, niece, to see if you've changed your mind. If you haven't, Hell will be your new home."

Laughing, he exited the room.

7

Sully continued to walk the streets until he heard footsteps behind him. He placed his hand on the hilt of his sword. He didn't look back but slowed his pace, listening. The footsteps were familiar. As he reached the corner, he stopped.

"Friend or enemy, Father? Which one are you?"

Asmodeus chuckled. "Your gifts will always amaze me. That gift is one of your mother's—protecting you, my son. I am your father, neither friend nor enemy. My goal is to see you succeed in your destiny, my son. A promise I made to your mother."

As Sully turned to face him, his shoulders dropped and his body relaxed. "I need Mick, Father. I need Katarina. I need them both at my side. Elias requires protection, but accepting my birthright hasn't brought me any closer to my destiny. I can't comprehend protecting both sides when only one is pursuing me."

The night air was cooler, but still humid. Las Vegas heat differed from Los Angeles, but Sully endured it. With his sword drawn, he strained to read the inscription by the dim streetlamp. A single tear slipped down his cheek as he traced the words. He knew the promise made between Heaven and Hell. He also recalled the promises he had made to Mick and Katarina. Before he could sheathe his sword, a woman's hand touched his arm.

A soft voice spoke. "My son."

Sully turned. "Mother."

Jophiel smiled at him.

He wanted to run to her, but he didn't. Stubborn, though his heart ached for her, he held back. He had grown up loving his adoptive parents, but when he needed guidance, it was Asmodeus who had always appeared—sometimes trying to force him down his path. In the end, Sully realized his father had only been preparing him to accept his true heritage and birthright. Looking at Jophiel, he smiled, though he stood his guard. She only ever visited in secret, or when Asmodeus was present. He couldn't comprehend their connection—whether pact-bound or genuine affection.

"Son, you can't just kill demons or angels. The pact that holds the balance between Heaven and Hell is the only thing preventing Lucifer from storming Heaven and slaughtering the innocent. Angels will not enter Hell. But there are leagues of rogue demons and angels, my son. Some on both sides no longer desire the pact. They long for the old war, thirsting for its return. Those are the ones you must stop from breaking it. You need to control your temper. I suppose you get that from your father." She chuckled, glancing at Asmodeus with a smile. He returned it.

Sully smiled faintly. "Mother, I am lost. I need both Mick and Katarina at my side. I don't understand why, but I'm lost without them. I care for both."

"Perhaps you're just disoriented, not lost. Michael fears for Mick. The longer she stays in Hell, the greater the risk she becomes the demons' toy. She risks everything if she doesn't leave, and Lucifer knows this. He agreed to the balance, but he cannot be trusted. Michael wants you to have this."

Jophiel handed him a small ornate blade. Gold, with an inscription on the handle that read *Protector* in the angels' language. Light as air in his hand, it gleamed with intricate design. The Soul Eater stirred, hungry, whispering: *How many demons can we kill with this?* Sully ignored him.

Jophiel continued. "Sully, your adopted name is John Sullivan. But the true name given to you by Michael was Raguel. Lucifer will give you a name as well. Your true name is incomplete until you receive the other from him. You need to ask Asmodeus to help you get Mick back. Katarina can help too. He has prepared for what lies ahead. Farewell, my son."

Before she could leave, Astaroth appeared and saw her. Sully stiffened, protective of his mother. Until now, no demon but his father had seen them together. The secret that kept her safe was at risk. His hand gripped his sword. He shifted to make sure Astaroth saw the blade gleam in the light. His father, too, stood protectively at Jophiel's side. Sully felt renewed determination as he observed their unspoken bond—mutual, and directed at him. But Astaroth could not see them together. The unthinkable was about to happen. It was time to play.

"Hunter." "Demon." "Who is this with you?" Astaroth sneered.

"She is not your concern," Sully said. "But my sword is, demon. Dance with me."

Astaroth jeered, showing no sign of backing down. He drew closer, and Sully braced for a fight. But instead of lunging, Astaroth revealed a small blade, angling it so Sully could read the inscription on the handle: *Power.* Could this be a blade from Lucifer?

"What's with the blade, demon?" Sully asked.

"Oh, hunter, you are a foolish one. Lucifer commanded me to give you this blade immediately. I had no choice but to obey. If I didn't have my orders, we would be fighting now."

Astaroth tossed the blade toward him and smiled. As Sully caught it midair, another demon appeared behind him and stabbed him with a second blade. Pain burned as steel pierced his side. Sully whirled to strike, but the demon vanished. He clutched his sword in one hand while pressing his wound with the other. Blood seeped, though at first he barely registered it. Minutes later, weakness spread through him.

"I did what Lucifer commanded," Astaroth said, "but I gave my own order to one loyal to me. I owed you that wound from before. I guess you could say we're even now, hunter." He vanished.

Sully tried to strike him but couldn't. His feet froze. His blood boiled, his insides melted—he felt like a cooking demon hunter. That's when the Soul Eater awoke. For the first time since their merge, it seized control against his will.

What the fuck was happening?

He couldn't move, though his sword was still in hand. Preparing for another attack, none came. He turned to Jophiel and mouthed *help,* though no sound left his lips. His gaze lingered on her as he collapsed. The Soul Eater was in control now, ravenous. Sully feared for his mother. They had allied—he prayed the Soul Eater would not betray it.

The voice thundered in his thoughts:*Hunter, someone poisoned us. But it was not meant for you—it was for me. Which demon did this?*

Sully answered silently."Astaroth came to show me a blade from Lucifer. One of his demons surprised me and struck. I trusted—because of her. I couldn't reveal her true identity. But Father will protect her if I cannot."

I already know your mother. We are one. Your thoughts are mine. To purge this poison, I must take control. If not, once it spreads, I will feed on your soul in seconds and annihilate you—and the pact will fall. We need Asmodeus. I will say goodbye for you to your mother. She must leave now.

Sully gave his mother a long, solemn look. He didn't want the Soul Eater speaking what might be his last words to her. He hoped she understood when he whispered, "You need to leave. Be safe. I will find you. I need Asmodeus. Poison."

The Soul Eater spoke aloud for him. "Angel, demons will come if you remain. The hunter needs his father before he dies. We will find you again, angel."

Jophiel nodded and vanished.

With the Soul Eater in control, Sully surrendered his will—to it, and to his father—to save him. He prayed it was not a mistake.

8

Asmodeus brought Sully back to the apartment where Elias and Edward were waiting. He cleared the table and laid his son down. Speaking in the demonic tongue, he asked the Soul Eater what to do.

Sully's lips parted, and the Soul Eater responded through him. "The poison. Someone intended to use the poison to destroy your son. You must bring us back to Hell. Remember your oath to Lucifer. He is the only one..."

The Soul Eater's words trailed off, and Asmodeus looked at the others. Unsure if it was a trap, he found himself in a predicament. He had discovered Astaroth's schemes against Lucifer and Sully, yet unresolved details still baffled him. He couldn't leave Elias alone, nor could he bring him to Hell. And he needed Edward's help to move Sully. A prophet didn't belong in Hell—but there was no other choice. Sighing, he spoke to them.

"We must all go to Hell. That includes you, prophet. Edward, help me with your brother. I need to get word to Lucifer. Elias, come here. I need to invoke my protection on you, and your side should comprehend. I want no retribution on me. You understand, prophet?"

Elias nodded and stepped forward. Asmodeus drew a blade, sliced his palm, and clasped Elias' hand. Then he pressed his bloody palm to the prophet's forehead and invoked his vow of protection upon Elias—for eternity. It had to be eternal for his son to succeed.

Asmodeus transported them all to Hell—specifically to Lucifer's lair, where they found Mick and Lucifer in hushed conversation. Asmodeus' eyes burned with fury toward his lord and liege, but something felt off. He had promised Michael to ensure Mick's safety—even from Lucifer—once Sully revealed her identity.

"Lucifer! The hunter needs you. The Soul Eater needs you. Both are one through their own choosing. To save one, you must save the other. One of Astaroth's demons poisoned the Soul Eater in retaliation six months ago. Save them—and then you'll tell me what you're doing with Mick!"

Lucifer appeared before them and sniffed the air in disgust. As his sly smile spread, Asmodeus returned a stern look, careful in case the others guessed at their deception. Only he and Lucifer knew their plan required bold moves to make it appear they were scheming against Sully.

"More of them? All these good people in my dominion? Where's the hunter?"

Asmodeus led Lucifer to an unconscious Sully, whom Edward had laid on the rock floor. While Lucifer worked his power over Sully, Asmodeus sent Edward a silent command to retrieve Mick. Elias shifted uneasily, glancing around their surroundings. Lucifer soon looked drained, which was unusual.

"My lord, what is wrong? Can you not heal them?"

Lucifer glanced back, swallowing hard. His usual regal composure had slipped—his face now weary and disheveled. When Mick arrived, she ran straight to Sully.

"Sully! What happened?"

She turned on Lucifer and Asmodeus, pounding her fists against him without resistance. Asmodeus realized the poison was too strong—even for Lucifer—and it wasn't his doing. If the poison took over, the Soul Eater would destroy Sully.

"Lucifer! The poison!"

Lucifer scowled. "It's one of Abaddon's. She tampered with my Soul Eater. Damn woman! Niece, do you care for the hunter?"

Mick hesitated, then nodded.

"Asmodeus, we need Katarina. I will command her here."

With a grim look, Asmodeus knew Lucifer had summoned her. He signaled Edward—once Sully recovered and the women were safe, they would leave Hell. Asmodeus would stay behind to keep the plan intact. Sully needed his strength to continue his investigations and prepare for what was coming. Edward nodded just as Astaroth appeared, making Lucifer seethe.

"You think to leave before we talk, Asmodeus? I have unfinished business with the women," Astaroth sneered.

Mick trembled, but Asmodeus moved to shield her. Before he could reassure her, Katarina appeared, confused—then furious.

"Who dares threaten Mick? She is under my protection, and I answer to no one."

Lucifer chuckled. "I summoned you, demoness. You will cure the poisoned Soul Eater, as I command. In exchange, you will protect Mick. Fail, and you face the wrath of my hellhounds."

"I am yours to command—but healing comes at a price. Hunter or not, it will cost you to save the Soul Eater."

Lucifer nodded silently. Asmodeus could sense his anger toward Astaroth. With a quick, powerful strike, Lucifer slapped Katarina, sending her sprawling. Asmodeus watched Astaroth's face—unmoved, emotionless.

Lucifer's voice thundered. "I still rule this dominion. I expect obedience. Demoness—heal the Soul Eater. Then meet me in my chambers with Astaroth and Asmodeus. Am I understood?"

Asmodeus frowned as the two women exchanged puzzled looks. What was Lucifer planning now?

Lucifer ordered Asmodeus to follow him into an adjoining chamber. Once there, Asmodeus warded the room against intruders and traps. He was finding it harder to maintain appearances while secretly working with Lucifer to shield his son and dismantle Astaroth's schemes. Tormented by divided loyalties, he couldn't fully grasp the cost of their deception. Oddly, Lucifer now looked as strong as ever—no trace of weakness.

"Lucifer, tell me what the fuck you're doing! And I want Abaddon's head on a platter."

Lucifer chuckled. "Prince Asmodeus, you are the fool. It's all part of my plan. Don't you see? The Soul Eater is safe. The poison is gone. But more is at stake—especially concerning my niece. Michael is not to be trusted. He gave her to the hunter so he would fall for her, keeping Heaven one step ahead of me. You have a choice, Asmodeus. Make your hunter love the demoness as well. The pact requires balance. If he does not, he will be mine—an eternal servant in Hell. He will become a Soul Eater."

"You can't do this! My son will not be your servant!"

"How dare you use that tone with me, Asmodeus! This is my dominion, and I am Lucifer, King of Hell! You owe me everything. Do not forget my true self."

Asmodeus realized Lucifer's raised voice was for Astaroth, who lingered outside, listening. He slipped into character, aware their plan depended on convincing the others they were divided. Neither Heaven nor Hell could afford to lose the hunter; if they did, rogue demons would annihilate both kingdoms—and humanity with them. Only Sully's adoptive family knew the truth.

"I know my place in your kingdom," Asmodeus said loudly. "Sully will obey."

In a hushed tone, he and Lucifer plotted to get Sully and his friends out of Hell before Astaroth stirred more rebellion. The pact had to be upheld. The rogues had to be rooted out. Despite his distrust, Asmodeus knew there was no choice but to follow through. He turned and left to face the others.

9

Astaroth learned Sully had finished his recovery in Asmodeus' chambers. He stared at Abaddon in a frenzy. Before she could speak, Astaroth raised his hand to slap her for her sloppiness. As his hand neared her face, Abaddon caught his wrist and flung it back at him. Astaroth seethed.

"Stupid bitch! Your poison should've worked on the hunter. He's healed now—and stronger than ever—with the damned Soul Eater on his side."

Abaddon laughed. Astaroth's patience with her arrogance was wearing thin, though he remembered what she'd promised before. Could she really deliver the hunter? He wasn't sure anymore, especially after what he overheard in Lucifer's chambers. They would have to move faster, and Abaddon had to prove herself. He turned and stormed off to find Beelzebub and Balam. Damn it.

On the way, Astaroth summoned several of his demons. "Our plans have changed. No one can meet my expectations. I will capture the prophet myself and bring the hunter to his knees. Find Balam and drag his worthless self to me now. Release the hellhounds into the world. Let them spread fear and collect souls until the hunter bows. Only then will I be unstoppable. Hell will belong to me! The hunter—and this pact—will reduce Lucifer to nothing."

The demons obeyed, unleashing hellhounds upon the world. Astaroth's dominance was only a matter of time. Within minutes, they had Balam bowing before him, surrounded by his fury.

"Grab the girl and unlock every secret in her mind. Find what she hides. Destroy the hunter. You have three days before I act against you."

Balam swallowed hard.
"Astaroth, what are you doing? She's protected. Lucifer knows who she is now."

"Incompetent fool! That means we must control her without Lucifer knowing. Bring her to me. I want the secrets in her mind. You failed the first time."

Balam left, though Astaroth noticed his trembling hands. Was he going to obey—or betray him? He'd have to keep a close eye on Balam. Abaddon, Balam, and the others were starting to become liabilities.

***

Mick paced the floor, clinging to Katarina. The more she thought of Lucifer as her uncle, the more disgust welled inside her.
"We must get out of here, Katarina. Something inside me is screaming for us to leave. I don't know what Lucifer meant, but is there a connection between us and Sully? He promised you only one night—and now Lucifer makes his own claim."

Her fury showed in her voice, though she chose her next words carefully. Locking eyes with Katarina, she spoke firmly.

"You promised to look after me, and I expect you to keep your word. You promised Asmodeus. We're trapped, but we must leave immediately."

As she said it, warmth spread inside her, power rising. Mick kept it hidden, not ready to admit what was happening. She gripped Katarina's arm, almost pleading. Katarina's eyes shifted, as if a realization had dawned. She patted Mick's hand in reassurance.

"Mick, we're not safe here. Something's wrong. I only want Sully to keep his promise—but he's yours. You're my friend now, and I won't betray you. But I don't trust anyone here anymore. Something's not right. I think we're in danger."

"Then help me. There's something inside me—strange. I feel strong in a way I don't understand, but I'm..." Mick lowered her voice to a whisper. "I'm the daughter of the archangel. I don't think I can survive in Hell."

Before she could say more, her body burned. She clutched her stomach and doubled over. A brilliant light engulfed her, banishing the darkness of the room. Asmodeus came running, but Mick noticed a shadowed figure nearby—it wasn't any of her allies. Was it Astaroth, or another demon?

Katarina steadied her, but the figure hurled fireballs. One struck Katarina, knocking her down, while Asmodeus turned to fight. Amid the chaos, Mick didn't see the advancing demons until too late. One pinned her arms, another injected her with something. Fire spread through her veins—then blackness.

When she woke, groggy, Balam loomed above her. She was bound to a table. The ropes bit into her skin with every movement. Fear gnawed at her. She bit her lip until blood trickled at the corner of her mouth.

She understood enough demonic words, thanks to Sully, to realize he was chanting. The same chant as before. He was after her mind. Mick resisted, fighting his intrusion, but her energy waned. Awake this time, she tried to shield what her father had told her. Dread filled her as her eyes locked with Balam's. She tried closing her eyes, but something inside her forced speech in a voice not her own—her father's voice.

"Daughter, protect yourself. The barriers won't hold for long *and once* he breaks through, the demons will know the secret you *protect*."

Despite her confusion, she sensed warmth in her right hand and twisted her wrist as far as possible. She aimed her palm at her captor. A red ball of fire flew past her and struck Balam, knocking him to the ground.

Her breath grew deeper as she opened her eyes, scanning the room to find Balam on the ground. She aimed her palms at the ropes and prayed that she could free herself. A ball of fire passed through her fingers, but the ropes stayed. Then she noticed Balam stirring and making his way back to the altar on all fours. Tears flowed from her eyes as she held them shut in fear of what he would do next. Mick was failing her father. Before Balam could get closer, she tried to close off her mind to everything in Hell through meditating. Though futile, it remained her sole hope Soul Eater would approach. She wasn't sure if her connection to Sully was strong down here, but the Soul Eater was her best chance to survive.

Balam was once again standing over her, his breathing loud and drops of his spit fell on her face. As she could sense what was going on, she was trying hard to protect whatever secret her father placed in her mind. Unsure of her correctness, she committed to resisting him as much as possible. Balam's power was entering her mind again, breaking through the barriers and with each one broken, Mick could feel the pain in her body radiating with sharp stings that only left her screaming in agony.

Her mind was crumbling. She could feel Balam's presence getting stronger while his breathing quickened. As Balam penetrated her mind, Mick felt the final barrier shatter as her mind crumbled, forcing her to cough and heave. As she laid there, she felt all her physical strength and courage break, causing her to scream in agony. Balam was making his move to enter her mind and gain access to her secret, but before he could start, a loud voice thundered across the chamber:

"Demon, obey—and retreat from the woman, as commanded."

Mick recognized the voice just as darkness overtook her.

***

Soul Eater had taken control. Sully could only watch as Balam was slammed against the wall, lifted by his throat, legs thrashing in the air. For the first time since their alliance, Sully felt the raw, cunning power of the Soul Eater. He laughed inwardly as the voice spoke through him.

"Dance with me, demon. Or would you rather face Lucifer?"

"Soul Eater, I obeyed your command. The woman is unharmed. Let me go."

"Fool. I am not only Soul Eater but Sully. We are one. Confusing, isn't it—for something as foul as you? You're not fit to serve Lucifer or belong in Hell. I wonder how your soul tastes. Shall we find out?"

Balam clenched his fists, still dangling. Soul Eater tightened his grip, inhaled, and savored a taste of Balam's soul. Balam screamed. Soul Eater took more, then dropped him to the ground.

He turned to Mick, lying unconscious on the altar, wounded from the attack. Placing a hand on her forehead, he glimpsed into her mind. The barriers shielding the archangel's secrets had been shattered. He and Sully worked quickly to reseal them—though only partially—hoping it would wake her. But she remained still.

With a heavy heart, he lifted her into his arms and walked away, leaving Balam broken on the ground.

10

Astaroth followed the demons and watched as they unleashed the Hellhounds into the mortal world. He stayed in the shadows, silent, until he noticed Abaddon approaching them. To avoid being noticed, he moved farther from the opening but stayed close enough to hear.

She whispered to the demons, her voice low, mumbling words Astaroth strained to catch. He inched closer. A few words reached him—and they made his blood boil. That vile demon! She had no intention of keeping her end of the deal. She planned to destroy them all and claim herself as Lucifer's right hand.

He watched as the demons left first, followed by Abaddon. Emerging from the darkness, Astaroth clenched his fists. These wayward demons needed to be brought back under his control. He would make one more attempt with the woman. But this time, he wouldn't use Balam, and Beelzebub's loyalty was questionable.

One demon could do what the others feared: Behemoth. The most feared in Hell next to Lucifer, and only God Himself could kill him. Astaroth knew that secret, thanks to his place in Lucifer's triad. Behemoth served for a price—one that might suit him. If Astaroth could find him, persuade him, Behemoth could undo everything that had been set in motion.

He left Hell to seek the Demon Behemoth.

***

Sully kept vigil over Mick, waiting for her to wake, but she didn't. Days had passed since the rescue. Soul Eater had gone silent after Sully allowed him to drink demons' blood. The prophet, too, was fading—the longer Elias stayed in Hell, the weaker he grew. Sully couldn't bear to watch his friend suffer.

He sought his father and Edward. "Father, the prophet must leave Hell. He won't be of use to me if he stays."

Asmodeus placed a hand on his shoulder. "Son, Katarina can help me care for Mick. Lucifer told me Astaroth released his hellhounds into the world above. Lucifer commanded them back, but they disobeyed. This has never happened before. The hounds always follow their master. Astaroth is plotting—and we cannot expose him."

"What do you mean? You and Lucifer are up to something. What is it? You know the rules, Father—I can't choose sides. My destiny, my birthright—remember? If I'm to trust you, you'd better start telling me the truth now."

Edward stepped forward, ready to stand with Sully. But Sully motioned him down and stood tall, radiating his authority toward Asmodeus. The demon prince gazed at his son, stepping back in amazement, unwilling to speak the truth.

Sully's fury flared. His temper awakened Soul Eater. Without hesitation, they merged, his eyes shifting—one yellow, one blue.

In a voice infused with Soul Eater's power, Sully thundered:"The prophet and I are leaving Hell. We'll return Lucifer's dogs to him. After that, I'll bring Mick back. Till then, protect her—and make her wake. Tell me the truth now, or suffer my anger."

Asmodeus stepped back and sighed heavily, fists clenched. Soul Eater allowed Sully to speak while watching in silence. Their alliance was no longer unholy but necessary for the pact.

"As you've discovered your identity and accepted your birthright, both kingdoms have begun to quake. Since the beginning, some opposed the pact—Astaroth, Balam, Abaddon, and others. When the two kings agreed, they feared rebellion. Michael always had a contingency. His daughter. She ensures your destiny, that you never forsake your purpose.

"Your journey began with finding the key. The next part will be harder. The book holds answers—but only when you're ready. Remember that, son. And know we are not alone. Spies are everywhere. The hounds are loose in the mortal world. They will devour men's souls and bring them here, feeding Lucifer's dominion, while their masters seize Hell. They seek to raise a faction against him—to replay the old war. But this time, their goal is annihilation. Both kingdoms destroyed. Humanity wiped out. They don't care.

"They'll use the prophet to control you. They'll pry into Mick's mind. The secrets she carries belong to both kingdoms. She's safe while unconscious—but not forever. You must save her. First, though, return the hounds. A hellhound can obey any demon—but once they defy Lucifer, no one is safe. Protect the pact. Do you understand, my boy?"

Sully was left disheartened and angry, more confused than before. He realized he had no choice but to hunt the hellhounds to stay on the path toward his destiny—whatever it was. Quietly, he spoke with Soul Eater, planning to leave his father behind to guard Mick. If there were rogues plotting to topple Lucifer and destroy the pact, someone had to preserve the balance. That burden fell to him.

Soul Eater came forward, letting Sully watch through his eyes. "Asmodeus, hear me. You and my mother don't get to choose my path. I'll honor my birthright—but my destiny is mine. Edward, choose now. Come with me or remain in Hell. Elias and I will track the hounds. Mick must be well when I return. I'm done with your games, Asmodeus. Tell Lucifer to stay out of my way."

The words stung Sully's heart, but they had to be spoken. If Astaroth was listening, he would believe them. Deep down, Sully hoped his father understood—Edward was needed at his side, and Mick had to be protected at all costs.

As he turned to leave, Sully glanced back. Asmodeus gave a single nod. Edward joined him, and together they set off to find Elias.

11

Asmodeus stood watch over Mick like a protective father while Lucifer paced the room. Though he was used to Lucifer's lack of patience, he had never seen the King of Hell so furious. For the first time, Asmodeus feared demons openly defying Lucifer's pact.

"Asmodeus, what's the hunter doing?"

He looked around before answering, choosing his words carefully. Only he understood the subtle hints his son had left before setting off to search for the hounds. While Asmodeus still had faith in Lucifer, he hesitated when it came to Mick's safety. He decided to gamble.

"The hunter knows what to do. I agreed to let Edward remain at his side. With him and the prophet, they may succeed. Mick, however, is compromised. I fear Balam affected her worse than before. Her secrets are no longer shielded by Michael. I believe Balam uncovered them before she was rescued. Somehow she called out to Soul Eater—and not the hunter. We need to know what Soul Eater knows, but he's not here."

Lucifer paced until he stopped in front of Mick. She looked peaceful in sleep. Asmodeus watched as Lucifer placed his hand over her temple.

What is he doing? He can't uncover her secrets. Lucifer smiled faintly, eyes closed. Then he turned, grim-faced. From a single glance, Asmodeus knew something had deeply unsettled him—a rare thing for the ruler of Hell.

As he remained silent, Asmodeus had no choice but to press him for answers. Lucifer refused to speak. After minutes of silence, he spoke at last.

"Where is the hunter? If Balam knows her secrets, both kingdoms are in danger. And Astaroth—he's released the hellhounds upon the world. Despite being King of Hell, my dominion will fall if they are not returned. Worse, Astaroth seeks an alliance with Behemoth. If that happens, everything the two kingdoms worked to protect will be destroyed. Not even your son can stop it—unless we wake Mick. She is the key to your son's destiny, according to my brother."

Asmodeus flew into a rage. The situation spiraled, no good outcome in sight. *How in hell is Sully supposed to capture the hounds?* His hand reached into his pocket. He pulled out the golden cloth Jophiel had given him long ago, saying, *If anything happens to Mick, open this and prepare our son.* He cursed himself for not realizing sooner.

Unwrapping the cloth, he found a tiny folded paper. He unfolded it and read the words—written in both angelic and demonic script. He muttered the demonic words to himself, then handed the paper to Lucifer with a whisper. "Oh, shit."

Lucifer's eyes widened. He trembled as he read. To Asmodeus' shock, the King of Hell fell to his knees. "What are you doing? Rise before other demons see the King of Hell quivering like a coward."

"The pact is destroyed," Lucifer said hoarsely. "Balam unlocked her secrets. Sully's path just became harder. We must act now, destroy those demons. Even though I desire Heaven's throne, I know the importance of balance and the pact. I have conceded to my brother in this—though he doesn't know it yet. I need my hounds. Sully must find them."

Before Asmodeus could answer, Abaddon stormed in, seething. Her rage was wild, unprovoked. Lucifer met her fury head-on, striking her across the face.

CRACK!

She touched her cheek, glaring at him. Asmodeus shifted his weight, ready for a fight.

"You may be King of Hell," she hissed, pointing at Lucifer, "and you may be Prince of Demons," she spat at Asmodeus, "but you will not stop Astaroth and the others. That girl's secrets are no longer hidden. Balam shared them with us all. Your end is coming. Both of you will die. And that son of yours will learn his fate soon enough. The pact will die with you. You will—"

She never finished. Lucifer hurled her into the wall. Her body crumpled, lifeless. He stepped over her as Asmodeus followed.

Lucifer quickened his pace, and Asmodeus struggled to keep up. His mind raced back to the cloth and Jophiel's warning. He trusted her—because, though he rarely admitted it, he loved that angel. And he loved his sons. Despite children by other demons and mortals, Sully and Edward held a special place in his heart—for they had embraced their true selves and their heritage without fear.

"Lucifer, where are you going?"

"Don't stop me, demon prince. I'm going to find every last one of them—starting with Astaroth. They will learn what it means to defy me."

***

The hounds prowled the mortal world, sniffing and searching for their target. Lesser demons followed under Astaroth's orders. Cerebrus, Raphael, and Eve stalked quietly, their paws padding in the shadows.

Astaroth couldn't afford failure. He gave his command to Abalam, and the demon knew the price of disobedience. Astaroth's wrath was legendary.

He motioned for his servants to follow at a distance from the hounds. Soon they spotted a man slumped against a building, tangled hair framing his face. He reeked of despair, a scent that lured hellhounds like blood. Astaroth watched eagerly.

Cerebrus circled the man. The mortal's eyes widened in terror as Raphael joined in. The hounds remained invisible until they found a soul marked for Hell—but Astaroth had changed the rules.

When the man opened his mouth to scream, Eve lunged, her jaws clamping his throat. His body convulsed as she shook him, and the three hounds vanished, dragging their prey to Hell.

The other demons looked at one another, uneasy. None had ever seen hellhounds disobey Lucifer. "Let's return to Hell," one muttered. "The mortal world is not for us."

The others nodded and they returned to Hell. Abalam remained behind as if something was troubling him. The other demons weren't needed as far as he was concerned. Then Abalam saw it. A strange hound replaced the familiar ones. He continued to sniff the ground then the air until something caught his attention. As the hound turned his head and looked at his surroundings, Abalam could hear his snarls, and it sent chills up the demon's back. Despite being a servant demon to one of the princes, Abalam lacked the ability to control a hell hound, so he had no choice but to obey Astaroth's commands, regardless of how they would affect Lucifer.

The hound disappeared, leaving a trail of black cloud smoke that was visible only to demons. Abalam followed carefully. Minutes later, he found the hound surrounded by mortals. More hounds appeared until Cerebrus and Raphael returned, claiming fresh prey for Astaroth.

"Shit. Lucifer's going to be pissed at Astaroth. But I don't serve Lucifer… This isn't right anymore. What is happening in Hell?"

Fear twisted his gut. He remembered standing near Balam as the hunter's woman was captured, her mind penetrated. The hunter's rescue had changed something in him, though he wouldn't admit it. Shaking the thoughts away, he kept watching as the hounds gathered under Cerebrus' command.

$$12$$

S ully and Edward wandered around town while Elias stayed behind to seek advice about the hellhounds being released. Sully didn't have time for games, and he wasn't in a good mood despite Edward's attempts to cheer him up. Upon reaching the middle of the Vegas Strip, they encountered a small demon horde—smaller in size but still menacing.

This is my luck!

Sully's face lit up. It had been some time since his last demon fight, and he embraced his destiny to keep the balance. He understood that engaging in a small "dance" with the horde wouldn't break the rules. It also gave him a chance to see what Edward could do since his return. With these odds, Sully's mood shifted. He reached for his sword as the demon horde stopped and faced them.

The dance was about to begin.

He curled his index finger toward the horde and flashed them a wide grin. Sully noticed Edward rolling his eyes as he readied his stance. Edward didn't reach for a weapon—instead, he flexed his biceps.

Hmm. This will be interesting.

Sully sighed. "Dance with me, demons. Come one, come all."

He had no intention of waking Soul Eater, but he knew the entity would be angry and likely feed on more of his soul as payback. Silently, he reached out to Lucifer's servant.

Want to play with demons, my unholy friend? Will you allow me to enjoy this moment alone?

Soul Eater replied, *Hunter, I think you deserve this dance alone. But afterward, offer me some demon blood. We need to save Mick.*

Agreed.

Sully hated the taste of demon blood, but he had no choice. Widening his stance, he gripped his sword in both hands and gave his wrist a twist. The blade came alive in a swirling dance. The demons watched in horror as Sully stepped closer.

"Shall I send you back to Hell?"

The demons split, some going for Sully and others for Edward. Sully smiled while Edward bent his neck from side to side, fists tightening. Sully saw his brother's muscles bulge and wondered what their father had been thinking when he transformed Edward into the muscle-bound demon beside him. Sully chuckled and refocused on his task.

The first demon stepped forward, slowly opening his hand to reveal a bright red-orange fireball. The flame rose and fell in his palm, unfazed. Sully remembered the angel and demon blades hidden in his boots—one in each. His sword continued spinning circles in his hand, forcing the demon to watch his swordplay. With a quick motion, Sully reached into his right boot and drew the angel blade. Holding both weapons, he circled the demon, closing the distance to the demon in a circle. As he did this, he noticed Edward and his small group of demons fighting but he didn't have time to watch his brother.

One demon made his move. But not with a fireball. He came running at him, head on, like he was a bull. With a smirk, Sully angled his angel blade and turned his left foot slightly and extended his right leg forward, preparing for contact. As the demon barreled into him, Sully used the angel blade to cut deep into the demon's side, causing him to fall hard into the blade. The demon's hands reached for the blade as the sheer look of horror made Sully's smile grow wider. Upon seeing the demon ablaze, the other demons froze as Sully's words rang out, "Who dares to dance with me next?"

The other demons shrank back in fear . Sully turned toward Edward—only to stop in his tracks, then erupt in laughter.

Edward, transformed and muscle-bound, was *bowling* with demons. He hurled their bodies one after another down the sidewalk toward a makeshift set of pins made of sticks and stones.

Sully whispered to Soul Eater, *Wake up. Look at what my brother is playing. Do you want their blood—or the one I killed?*

Soul Eater stirred. Sully's eyes shifted blue and yellow, Sully focused his vision on Edward bowling with the demons. Soul Eater chuckled and said, "*I will drink from them all. Let's go.*"

Sully sighed as he once again, relinquished control to Soul Eater and as the demon emerged from within, Edward's attention turned towards him.

"Soul Eater, you are back. I can sense those yellow eyes anywhere. Are you bloodthirsty, friend?"

Soul Eater, now in control, moved closer and fed on the demons one after another. Blood trickled down Sully's chin and onto his shirt, but nothing could stop the entity from savoring its feast. Licking Sully's fingers clean, Soul Eater enjoyed the tart taste.

Edward grinned and lifted the last demon, untouched. "You forgot one."

By the time he finished speaking, Soul Eater had retreated. Sully re-emerged, glancing down in disgust at his bloodied shirt, forcing down the lingering taste. This was one part of their alliance he loathed.

"Brother, he left that one for me."

Edward studied Sully's now-blue eyes. "Brother! How shall we handle this one? He's not entirely dead...yet."

"You had your fun, Edward. Now it's my turn. We must find those hounds—I suspect this one has crucial information about Mick. Toss him here."

Edward then grabbed the still demon, pulled back, and released it. Sully made the motion to catch him but then moved one step backward, letting the demon fall hard on the pavement, still motionless.

***

As Lucifer and Asmodeus paced the floor, Mick struggled to sit up. Her body felt weak and broken, but she knew something inside her had changed. She didn't know what—but when her eyes locked on Lucifer, she screamed. The sound sent both demons rushing toward her, fear on their faces.

Mick noticed Lucifer's dark eyes were damp, his demeanor shifted. He almost looked concerned. He reached for her face, but before his hand could touch her cheek, images flashed through her mind—of him and her celestial father.

"I...I...don't touch me. I see them—you and Michael. Why were you fighting together?"

The visions blurred, her head pounding. She hunched over, hands clutching her temples, speaking in the demonic tongue.

Lucifer grabbed her hands, and though she perceived comfort, something felt wrong. She tried to pull away but couldn't. Images filled her mind: Asmodeus holding a baby, Lucifer watching. Then Asmodeus's gaze shifted from the child to her. She was *in* the vision. Dizziness overwhelmed her.

"Help...help me."

Asmodeus laid her back down and Mick drifted to sleep once more. She could feel their hands checking her for signs of life or death but she couldn't respond anymore. She was trapped in her own mind, her own visions. She could only hear the voices outside her body but didn't understand the commotion. Mick was alone again and to make matters worse, ALONE IN HELL!

***

Katarina ran to Mick and started fuming. Her rage was no longer controllable. *If anything happens to her, the hunter will hold me responsible. I must save her, no matter what they command.*

She had many skills, one of which she'd kept hidden: a telepathic bond with Mick since Edward had dragged them both to Hell. Only Edward knew—his way of keeping his brother's love safe.

Katarina thought of the hunter and his promise to bed her. All she needed was one chance to create the child—the child that would change her future in Hell.

Placing a hand on Mick's temple, she turned to Lucifer, seething. "What the fuck did you do to her?"

Lucifer's eyes narrowed, his glare sharp. "I am the King of Hell. What gives you the right to speak to me like that, wench?"

His hand rose to strike her, but Asmodeus intervened. Katarina smirked before turning back to Mick. Closing her eyes, she reached through their bond, determined to destroy whatever plagued her friend.

Inside Mick's mind, Katarina sensed Balam's handiwork woven into her soul. The longer she stayed, the more suffocated she felt—but she pressed on. Then she saw it: a faint shadow, retreating whenever she approached.

Pushing forward, she summoned her power. The figure suddenly rushed at her. Startled, she gathered her strength. It stopped inches away, extending a bony hand with long fingernails. In its palm rested a key.

The figure spoke but it wasn't in the demonic language so Katarina knew that it wasn't something Balam left in her mind. It was something else. The hand shook as if it was waiting for her to take the object.

Katarina said, "Will that save Mick?"

The figure shook its hand once more and dropped the object into her hand before disappearing. Katarina had to get out of Mick's mind. Something was happening to her friend. She returned to her body and found herself starting at Asmodeus and Lucifer, who were asking a lot of questions she didn't know how to answer.

13

Abaddon roamed the world above, seething at the thought of betrayal by Astaroth and the others. They had lured her into a trap against Lucifer, one she hadn't seen coming. She had no quarrel with the King of Hell—only a desire to control the hunter.

Having taken the pitiful form of a human woman, her plan had become more deceptive. She needed the prophet, but to reach him, she first had to control the hunter. Wandering aimlessly, she soon caught his trail.

She spotted him fighting several demons alongside Asmodeus' other son, Edward. The two were dominating, though the fight was not yet decided. She hung back, watching, and noticed the hunter's eyes—Lucifer's servant had emerged, then slumbered again. She could use that to her advantage.

Abaddon remained quiet until she felt deep breathing on the back of her neck.

Her eyes flicked toward the sound. Cerberus.

Fear rose within her as the warm breath of the hellhound washed over her. She swallowed hard, knowing full well what such beasts could do.

Perhaps Astaroth—or another—wanted her dead more than the hunter. She clenched her fists and waited.

Cerberus spoke to her telepathically, delivering his news.

Abaddon smiled grimly when he finished. The hunter was his, and his alone, by order of Lucifer himself. Defeated once more, she crawled away but not before swearing to get even with everyone who prevented her from capturing the prophet in the end. It was only through her insight that she realized that the key to the hunter's fall was the prophet.

***

Forced on the ground, Elias found himself blindfolded and gagged for some unknown reason. The last he remembered, he had just parted from Sully to research something about the pact in one of the books they had been studying. His head throbbed, and something wet trickled down the side of his face.

He strained to listen to the voices around him—then another voice echoed in his mind.

The pact was made for a reason. The books contain only part of the answer until you merge your mind with the chosen daughter. She is the key to the hunter's destiny.

Elias nearly choked at the words but forced himself to remain still, feigning unconsciousness.

One of his captors spoke.

"The pact has done nothing for either side, and the hunter is more than he was before. Asmodeus protects him as he does Lucifer, and we need what's in his mind to free the others."

The others? Elias listened intently.

"What about Lucifer? We can't overthrow him if Asmodeus remains at his side. Asmodeus is our key to his undoing."

"Settle down, Balam. We've got the prophet, and Abaddon wants him too. We'll use him to bring the hunter to his knees. Abaddon can't be trusted, and neither can Katarina. We'll find a way to remove them both and destroy the hunter. Once he's gone, Lucifer will be ours."

Elias held still, desperate to hear more—but the inner voice returned.

The key from the garden is only the beginning. You must guide the hunter by surviving. Look for Heaven's door at the Shrine of the Redeemer, where the hunter resides. Enter through and speak to the angel who guards the way. Seek what is needed.

Cold hands gripped Elias's shoulders, hot breath brushing his face.

"Prophet, listen closely. If you don't want your worthless soul devoured by a hound, bring the hunter to us in three days. This is your only warning. Fail, and the hound will find you—and you know what they can do. Pray all you want, but deliver the hunter."

Elias stayed silent, his heart pounding. Before he could react, the world went black.

Hours later, he awoke in an abandoned alley with three demons standing guard.

"Look, the prophet's awake. Three days—that's your warning."

The demons vanished, leaving him alone in the night. He found a card in his hand and made out the symbol using the streetlight above. Astaroth. He gritted his teeth and stood up. Remembering the voice, he put the card in his pocket and searched for the church.

***

Michael sat in a familiar bar in Los Angeles, three hundred miles from the hunter and the prophet. This was the bar his daughter had once tended, the same place where she befriended the hunter and discovered her identity.

Sipping his gin, he smiled at the hand fate had played in the hunter's destiny. He had watched Sully grow into a man, unchanged and unmarked, until the day he accepted the sword and his birthright.

A hand touched his shoulder. He looked up to see Raphael and Jophiel joining him, one on each side. The three angels shared a knowing smile.

"Raph," Michael said, "the hunter is torn. My daughter remains among the demons, and the prophet has vanished. What news do you bring of the rogue angels? And the demons?"

Raphael clenched his jaw before speaking, his glass empty. "A handful of angels left Heaven and fell to earth. They are not 'fallen' in the usual sense, but the Lord has forbidden their return unless the hunter delivers them. Asmodeus and Lucifer are following Jophiel's plan to protect him. Our plan is working, but Mick's condition and the release of the hounds are making it harder to preserve the pact. Without it...you know the cost."

Michael shook his head. The pact was the balance binding Heaven, Hell, and the world together. Angels could not interfere directly, only assist when needed and watch. He had helped the hunter quietly throughout Sully's life, though Sully never knew. But this time was different. The prophet was missing, and Sully and his demon brother were locked in battle.

He sighed, feeling the weight of the world on his shoulders.

Turning to Jophiel, he raised his glass. He knew the angel beside him loved her son, yet she could only watch with his father and hope Sully would succeed.

Once Sully had the key, Michael knew, the gates of both kingdoms would open to him. The hunter's chosen alliances would either preserve—or shatter—the pact.

14

Sully and Edward sat at the table, combing through books until one tattered, leather-bound volume stood out from the pile. Though worn and aged, its pages looked crisp and fresh. Sully didn't pay much attention at first—until something compelled him to look closer. Intrigued, he picked up the book and examined it, noticing the mark of Asmodeus etched into the back right corner. He opened it and began to read.

When he finished the passage that caught his eye, he clenched his fist and slammed it against the table. The crack startled Edward, who stared at him wide-eyed.

"That bastard! Look here...look at this part. This is unfathomable—horrifying."

He jabbed a finger at the words. As Edward read, Sully's anger rose again. He had always kept his temper under control when killing demons, but this time he failed to keep his emotions in check.

Edward looked at him in pure shock, speechless. Then, in a firm voice, he said,

"This book belongs to Father. It was given to him long ago, and Lucifer considered it one of his most prized possessions. But I remember Father saying that when the pact was made, Lucifer wrote this book to guide him when the time came. Father never gave it a second glance because he knew he wouldn't need it—until you accepted your destiny."

"Edward, it speaks of another battle, but not the War in Heaven. This is the War in Hell—a second war, after Lucifer's expulsion. What is really happening down there?"

Edward stayed silent, staring at the floor. Sully studied his brother's demeanor before asking again, this time in a harsher tone—a tone he only used when sending demons back to Hell. Still, Edward said nothing. He only pointed to the book, forcing Sully to keep reading.

"Silent, little brother? Have it your way but I will get my answers from either you or the Soul Eater. One way or another."

Sully picked up the book and left the room to continue reading alone.

***

Katarina had listened to Asmodeus and Lucifer rattle through their questions and all she could do was smile. She wiped her brow , she scrambled for an explanation. She herself couldn't quite make sense of what had happened inside Mick's mind. A strange being had appeared, handed her an object, then vanished without a word. It sounded insane—but this was Hell. Anything was possible.

"Katarina," Lucifer growled, "minutes have passed and you've said nothing. We are waiting for answers. What happened in Mick's mind? Was she harmed by the demons?"

His horns glowed dark red—a sign that his rage was slipping beyond control. Katarina sighed, knowing this could turn ugly fast.

She placed her hand gently on Mick's temple.

"A figure entered her mind but spoke no words. It only gave me an object.

I don't know if it will wake her, heal her, or harm her. But Balam tampered with her mind—his traces are everywhere. My lord, if Mick truly is the daughter of the archangel Michael...shouldn't we consider asking him for help?"

Lucifer's mouth curled into a hard grin.

"You would invite the archangel Michael into my kingdom without breaking the pact? Foolish wench! I should strike you down for even thinking it."

Katarina shivered, waiting for Asmodeus to intervene. At first, he only stared at her as though she had misread what she saw. Then his expression softened, and he smiled.

His gentle voice broke the heavy silence.

"One step at a time, Katarina. I understand your friendship with Mick is unusual, but only a handful of individuals are central to the pact. You and Mick are included because of Sully. Your survival will depend on the alliances you choose."

"I don't understand. The presence in her mind wanted her to have this, but I'm afraid to make that choice for her. Mick is like a sister to me...even if we both love the Hunter."

Lucifer's cold voice cut in.

"Give me the item. I want to see what my niece is meant to take."

The word *niece* sent a chill through Katarina. His protectiveness—and that flicker of emotion—felt out of place for the King of Hell.

Asmodeus squeezed her shoulder reassuringly, and she reluctantly handed Lucifer the small, round object. She leaned close with them, watching as it rested in his palm.

The dark sphere gave off a pungent, sulfuric odor laced with iron. In humans this would be used to treat acne problems but to demons and angels, this would only result in welts.

Asmodeus reached for the ball and held it up. As Katarina fixated on the object that resembled a large circular pill, she noticed that its scent got stronger the longer it remained in Lucifer's hand. Minutes passed while they sat in silence, staring at it, until Lucifer's hand began to show blisters. In shock, Asmodeus grabbed it and held onto it until his hands began to blister. This time, Katarina grabbed the pill and placed it in Mick's right hand. The pill did not blister her hand, but it began to melt. She began to fear this response, so she knocked the remaining solid part of the pill out of her hand onto the floor.

"Something's wrong. Demons can't touch it, but it melts in Mick's hand. What the hell is this thing? We can't give it to her."

But before anyone could wipe her palm clean, the melted substance seeped into Mick's skin and vanished.

15

The three hell hounds stuck together as they roamed the streets of Vegas. It was clear to them that Cerebrus was the leader—the one Lucifer had put in charge. Cerebrus's orders were clear from the start and came directly from Lucifer: under no circumstances were they to obey his commands until they connected with the hunter, but they had to make Astaroth and the others believe they'd stopped listening to Lucifer for the plan to work.

Cerebrus used their special connection to communicate with Eve and Raphael. Images of the hunter were sent to the other hounds; their mission was to bring the hunter and the prophet to the location Lucifer specified. If any humans saw them, they were free to bring those humans to Lucifer for sentencing. He had already distracted Abaddon and now needed to search for the hunter.

Between Eve and Raphael, Cerebrus led the way through the streets until they reached a group of demons. From a distance he heard the demons whispering to a man who appeared to be hurt. Cerebrus told Raphael to watch them as he moved closer. Though intelligent and loyal to Lucifer, hell hounds were ruthless, vicious creatures. Cerebrus moved with stealth and, on closer inspection, saw that the man being tortured was the prophet. His lips moved, exposing sharp canines as drool dripped from his mouth. Cerebrus heard their demands and silently sent a report to Lucifer. Though forbidden to obey Lucifer's orders directly, they were instructed to keep him updated on their progress and on what the demons were doing.

The man vanished, but Cerebrus didn't follow—because a human had seen him and his demon instincts took over. Cerebrus dragged the screaming man straight to the depths of Hell and left him there.

***

Elias made his way to the Church of the Redeemer—known in Vegas as the Shrine of the Most Holy Redeemer. Though the shrine looked modern, the aura of the prophets spoke through its walls. He entered, and not long after a man approached.

The man was not dressed as a man of the cloth; he looked destitute, hair matted and face unclean.

"Friend, are you lost?" the man asked.

Elias remained silent, watching. As a prophet he knew better than to give away too much at once. The man looked him over and smiled, then spoke in the angelic language Elias loved. Sully rarely used it—he preferred the demonic tongue—so Elias felt a sudden ache for the company of the other prophets.

The man spoke of the hunter's destiny and the Second War, and Elias's interest sharpened. He wondered whether Sully knew about this Second War.

"Brother, tell me more about this Second War. The pact was meant to protect against this. I know God does not want this war, but Sully and I have separated for the moment to rescue the women."

"All I know comes from what I hear among demons. This disguise is perfect for eavesdropping. Ask what you must, prophet."

Elias sat in a nearby pew and waited.

"Friend, I was surrounded by Astaroth, Balam and others. They demanded I bring the hunter to them, but we were separated when the hunter was attacked. This Second War you speak of—does Lucifer intend to break the pact? The hunter swore his allegiance to it and formed a bond with Lucifer's servant. Only a few of us understand the intensity of that bond. If a war breaks out...annihilation could follow."

As the doors to the Shrine locked, the man's guise fell away. The walls began to glow; angelic script unfurled across stone, and a mosaic in the shrine's center lit with radiant light. A scroll inscribed *"Sanctus, Sanctus, Sanctus"* revealed a hidden image of the hunter's sword. The man was no longer destitute but the angel who had stood beside Elias since the pact was made.

Elias embraced his brother and listened. After hearing everything, he vowed to share the knowledge with the hunter and to find Sully and Edward. The angel warned him that demons were still demons—be wary of those who chose to serve and those who wished to destroy. Whatever choices were made, Elias swore to protect the hunter and to recognize the crucial importance of both women: should the hunter fall, the women must protect the pact. Elias needed to find the hunter and reunite with him and Edward as soon as possible.

***

Astaroth, Balam and Abaddon met in a shadowed alley, keeping to the dark. Abaddon had brought a few of her minions; Astaroth was annoyed but let it pass. More ears on the plan, he decided, wouldn't hurt—though he had warned her not to push her luck in this lifetime.

Balam was the first to break the silence after Astaroth's warning. "What if the prophet fails? How will we corner the hunter? The secrets I found in that little bitch's head are incredible—ripe for the taking. And the little surprise I planted inside her will serve our purpose."

Astaroth frowned. "What surprise?"

Balam smiled, and his look made Astaroth angrier still at what the two of them might do to ruin his plan. "Calm down, Astaroth. The seed is perfect because I know Asmodeus will use Katarina to try to fix the woman's mind. Katarina's power to enter minds is unfathomable and useful. When she enters, she'll see a figure that seems to help—but the surprise I left will make the woman lose control. Her connection to Heaven will slowly erode. It will be slow enough to lure the hunter into our grasp; once together, she will unleash her altered abilities on him, and he will fall under our control. Neither Lucifer nor Asmodeus will be able to stop us once we own the hunter. He will take commands from us and no longer have his own will."

Astaroth rubbed his chin, smirking. He wanted more details about what Balam had found in the woman's mind, but Balam remained coy. That silence only infuriated him further. Deep down, he wondered if his plan might finally succeed after all these centuries under the pact. Hell would reign on the mortal world, and the gates of both kingdoms would remain open forever.

"If you're that confident," Astaroth said, "then our faction may yet dominate this world. But if either of you fuck this up, you'll spend eternity serving me until I'm no longer satisfied. Only your death will end your suffering if you destroy my plan—especially you, Abaddon. While demons fear you, I do not. I have special use for you in my domain."

Abaddon stared and nodded. Astaroth enjoyed bending her to his will when he could. He knew she hated it, but it amused him. He was not afraid of Balam—Balam was a much lower demon, useful, and easily dispensable.

To Astaroth, either outcome—keeping him or estroying him—would sat-isfy. Destroying the pact was crucial, but overthrowing Lucifer was a far bigger dream. Now, at last, it felt possible. Astaroth intended to savor the moment.

16

Margaret O'Leary wheeled herself around the dark bar, waiting for her guest to arrive. Ever since Sully had paralyzed her, her mission to recruit him had shifted to revenge. Her family's organization would succeed in controlling him, forcing him to destroy all demons and angels that remained. Her father and uncle had reminded her of the plan countless times, but since that day battling Sully, she had never shaken her thirst for vengeance.

She had memorized his entire file and his recent activities, though the two women puzzled her. She recalled Mick, the human, but the second was a demoness—talented, and favored by Lucifer himself. By the look of their activities, she would be a handful.

Margaret's hands clenched into fists and she banged her right hand against the wheelchair arm. Just thinking about him filled her with hate—but when she remembered his strong features, dark hair, blue eyes, and that smile, her heart softened. The warmth lasted only a moment before her phone rang.

Her assistant handed her the phone, but Margaret noticed his eyes were fixed straight ahead, past her wheelchair. She turned her head and saw a horde of demons approaching. Her assistant raised his gun and aimed.

Margaret said, "If you don't want to be sent back to Hell to beg for your worthless lives, I suggest you stop and speak from there."

The demons stopped, and their leader spoke. "Sister, we come to serve you. Astaroth sent us."

"What do you mean by this?"

The demon laughed. "Foolish woman. Do you really think you can control the hunter on your own? Astaroth wants to make you an offer you can't refuse. Or you can keep wallowing in misery over what the hunter did to you."

Margaret turned to her assistant. "Lower the weapon, but stay ready. Kill them if they come too close. I'll hear them out, but I'm not stupid enough to trust the enemy."

The assistant lowered the gun. Margaret motioned for the demons to approach. It was a gamble, but one that might both satisfy her family's organization and fuel her revenge. Two birds, one stone. And Sully would be hers to control.

The leader came close enough to speak without shouting, but kept his distance. Margaret noticed his caution, and then recognized him—her eyes widened with suspicion. "You are the demon Bael. You never appear without reason. How are you in league with Astaroth?"

"Well, dear lady, that's an interesting story. Care to hear it? Or shall we tell Astaroth you no longer want the hunter?"

Her fists tightened in rage, but her assistant leaned down and whispered. "Miss, this is Bael—commander of many legions in Hell. He's formidable, with or without Astaroth. We could use him, and then use the hunter to destroy them all."

Margaret pursed her lips into a smile. Her assistant, Archer, had served her well ever since her uncle gave him to her. He had been with the organization since birth, carefully trained to serve. She had grown to rely on his strength, advice, and knowledge.

Bael leaned closer, though still at a safe distance. The little game amused her. He was toying with her, and she with him. She liked games like this.

"Listen closely," Bael said. "Astaroth already has a plan to capture the hunter and the prophet. The woman who captured the hunter's heart has been poisoned in her mind. There is no cure. The hell hounds no longer obey Lucifer. It's only a matter of time before the hunter is ours. The deal is simple: you can use the hunter for your purposes if you provide certain services for the demons. Make the requests Astaroth gives you, and you'll share him. When we tire of him, he'll be yours. A win-win."

"What services does my organization need to perform?"

Bael's smile widened, sinister. "Margaret, don't play stupid. You have access to human women and men. We need them to create children. Your organization claims to serve the Holy Church, but we know your secret—you destroy angels and demons. We simply want to change that. All you need do is destroy angels, because Astaroth will break the pact, giving our kind dominion over the world. You'll be our tools for control."

He paused. "If you refuse, the terms become less favorable. Talk to your father and uncle. Decide quickly."

The terms disgusted her. They were not part of her plan—or her father's. But the chance to control Sully was tempting.

"I'll send a message when I have my father's answer."

Margaret motioned for the assistant to wheel her back. Her mind was racing but she was torn, a feeling she would not admit to anyone.

***

Sully sat alone in one room, his brother in the other. He wasn't angry at Edward; as long as Edward had been with him, he'd always spoken truth as best he knew it. Maybe he really didn't know about the Second War. Or maybe Asmodeus had withheld the truth for a reason. What about his mother? Would she know?

Thoughts churned until he felt Soul Eater stirring.

The voice came, calm and calculated, as always.

"We are one, hunter. You either trust me, and I you, or this alliance destroys us both. Our fates are intertwined, though I serve Lucifer. He commanded me to devour your soul and forge our alliance, whether you accepted destiny or not. Will you trust me to help you? You may be surprised at what I know."

Sully was stunned, but something inside urged him to trust. Instinct, pure and simple. Perhaps this alliance was more valuable than he'd thought.

"Tell me what you know, my unholy friend. Will there truly be a Second War in this lifetime?"

"Friends, are we? Good. Listen well, hunter. The pact was never accepted by all. For ages the demons obeyed—until that fateful day you faced Lucifer's first soldier, Cain. Neither you nor Cain could die. Each strike only made you stronger. It was a no-win *situation*. Remember *that fight, my hunter* brother? Cain, *the first soldier,* convinced *certain* demons to *begin* factions *and* to one day start the Second War *between the angels and demons. This Second War will destroy* the pact, *break* the gates of *both* Heaven and Hell *open* and *set* the *Hell Hounds loose on* man. There will be no light, only darkness. *The world of man* will *forever be in dark,* barely *surviving, and the only ones in control will be* the victors *of the war.* When you fought Cain, you triggered something *inside you that Cain sought to destroy. Your* destiny. Only *Cain has that power* because he *is the one* born *from* both sides, *like you.* You and Cain are equals *in a way.*"

"Cain? You mean *Cain,* the son of Adam? That Cain?"

Sully wasn't sure if Soul Eater meant the Cain of scripture or another demon who bore the name. He waited for an answer, rubbing his side. Since the last battle, the wound there had never healed. That alone troubled him. Normally, no matter what came his way, he healed quickly. But this—this lingered. He'd told no one. Not Edward. Not even his father.

"My brother. My friend. Yes, *that* Cain. Son of Adam and Eve. Destroyer. Wicked one. The Mark of Cain forbids his death, but he bargained with Lucifer and became his first soldier. He commands legions in Lucifer's name. Obeying him is like obeying Lucifer himself. He holds more weight than many lords of Hell. Neither you nor he can kill the other. That day you fought him, it was useless. You both were injured. There was no victor. But Cain will lead the factions against Heaven in the Second War."

Sully tried to absorb the words, recalling the day he fought Cain. The man had been unlike any opponent—formidable, powerful, his swordwork in eerie sync with Sully's own. At times, it had felt less like fighting and more like a mirrored dance. Since that day, he had not seen him again. But Soul Eater's words lingered.

Would Cain return? Sully didn't know. But dread settled deep in his stomach. His instincts told him yes—he would see Cain again.

17

Mick began to stir after her skin absorbed part of the pill. Her eyes remained closed, but she could hear everything being said. Whatever she had absorbed, it made her feel strange. She tried to move her arms but couldn't.

"Mick, Mick. Are you awake?"

She recognized Katarina's voice, but she couldn't respond. Her insides burned with a heat she had never felt before. Pain radiated through her body, and her mind screamed with unbearable intensity.

As she suffered in silence, thoughts of her father and the secrets she held shattered. Whatever they had given her was changing her. Mick needed a way to make them stop, but she didn't know how. Her memories felt broken—removed, destroyed—she couldn't tell which. But she knew she was losing something important. Her father had made her the keeper of those secrets. They mattered. Her destiny was to help the hunter—so what had they done to her? Damn demons.

Then she heard his voice. Her familial connection to him might be the key. Lucifer. Uncle Lucifer.

Niece, use your power to speak to me. You are not only human. Remember that. You carry the bloodline of Michael, the archangel. Use it. I feel your pain through the bloodline.

Mick wasn't sure she understood, but she tried. She thought her words and sent them to him, praying they would reach.

Uncle Lucifer. Help me. My body is burning, and the secrets Father gave me are disappearing. I can't wake up, but I can hear you. I think I need you, but I don't know what's happening. I feel the light fading. Help me.

She waited, desperate. Seconds stretched into minutes until Lucifer's voice broke through again.

Niece, this is bad. This reeks of Balam's doing—to destroy you and the hunter. Katarina entered your mind and brought out a pill from a strange force. We didn't know what it would do, but part of it melted into your skin. The rest is here with me. Its effects are clearly disastrous. I can't counter it. The secrets must not be lost. Even I can't know them—nor do I want to. I trust my brother and the pact, or I would never have agreed to it. Niece, this is not my doing, but I may have to contact Michael. The archangel and I might have to work together to save you. I will send for the hunter to return to Hell. I need you to trust me, niece. I am going against my nature for you, child."

Mick was devastated but upon hearing the sincerity in her uncle's voice, she had no choice but to trust him.

***

Lucifer sent for one of the hell hounds, a soul retriever he trusted. Ramses. Silent, patient, deadly—the perfect hunter. He motioned Asmodeus to his side, away from Katarina and Mick, and spoke in low tones.

"Listen closely, Asmodeus. This can't leave us. Not your sons. Not anyone."

He paused, waiting for Asmodeus's nod before continuing.

"I'll command Ramses to stand at Heaven's gate. My hope is to lure Michael out. Once he's outside, I'll appear. We need his help to save the woman—my niece. You will guard against any interruption, demon or otherwise. If we don't save Mick, the pact will fall, your son will be destroyed, and the world along with him. And I'll suffer the backlash of these upstart demons. If the pact is broken, it will be by me or my father—not by lowborn demons who can't stomach the hunter's birthright."

Asmodeus nodded. Lucifer could always count on his loyalty. That was why he had chosen him for the pact—though Lucifer never admitted it. His rage simmering, Lucifer used his mind to command Ramses. The hound vanished instantly to obey.

"Let's go, Asmodeus."

Before leaving, Lucifer ordered Katarina to protect Mick at all costs, handing her his personal blade. He withheld the rest—things in Hell were spiraling too far out of control. If either woman died, the hunter would lose his mind, and neither Heaven nor Hell would survive. This much Lucifer knew. The balance the pact brought stemmed from the Hunter's control. As Lucifer and Asmodeus left, Lucifer began to wonder if the pact was worth it but the benefits the agreement brought led him to control his kingdom without having to obey his father or brothers. A price he was willing to pay.

***

Ramses stood at Heaven's gate, waiting patiently. The guarding angel shifted uneasily at his presence. When Ramses let out a long howl, the angel recoiled in fear and blew his horn. Ramses knew then he had succeeded—he had Michael's attention.

Lucifer's command was simple: do not attack, only draw the archangel out.

But another voice pressed into Ramses's mind. Cerebrus, commanding him to help find the hunter. Torn, Ramses chose Lucifer's command instead.

Brother, the lord commanded me on a different task. I fear I can't obey you. After I will hunt."

All the hellhounds knew that disobeying their lord Lucifer would result in death in one of the pits and no hound wanted that because in those pits lived the souls they hunted, and they all knew that those tortured souls would unleash their anger on the hounds, causing eternal suffering. That was the secret of the hounds and a way to destroy them without killing. No man has yet been able to kill a hound.

Ramses watched until he saw the magnificent archangel appear at the gates. The angel tilted his head to the left and then to the right until Ramses saw his face harden but he never spoke. As the angel watched the hound, the hound let out a small growl, followed by two sharper growls. Michael's lips tightened.

"Take me to your master."

Ramses turned and led the way to where his lord was waiting.

***

Lucifer motioned for Asmodeus to remain back in the shadows but on guard. He stepped out from the shadows and into the light. Michael approached. Silently, he ordered Ramses back to Asmodeus with a deadly command: *Kill anyone who interrupts, even Asmodeus. Kill.*

Michael came close, and Lucifer spoke. "Your daughter is quite popular with my demons, brother."

Michael's eyes flashed. "Harm one hair on her, and you will feel my sword."

Lucifer laughed. "She is my niece. I won't harm her—but she is in danger. One of the demons harmed her, and I need your help to save her. Will you trust me, just once?"

As he spoke, Lucifer was already planning. It was too early for the women to rejoin the hunter. His hold over Katarina was incomplete, especially after seeing her bond with Mick. He needed Katarina to sire a child with the hunter—a child bound to him, not the world. The hunter had to be manipulated carefully, and Katarina was perfect for it. Mick stood in the way, but Michael could deal with her. Soft spot or not, Lucifer would bury it.

Michael stayed silent, and Lucifer grew impatient. "Michael, will you help me save her or not?"

"She's my daughter. I'll help—but she's in your kingdom. What do you expect me to do?"

Lucifer considered. Detoxifying Mick, finding the hunter—these were the next steps. But angels could not enter Hell under any circumstance. For once, Lucifer found himself at a loss...and reluctantly deferred to Michael's ideas.

$$18$$

S ully was bored, and his muscles ached for a fight. He was frustrated that the women were in Hell and not at his side. As he gripped his sword's handle, he felt the faint vibrations of his connection with it—and the hunger of the Soul Eater once more. The hunger was sharp, insistent, and not easily satisfied.

"Soul Eater, hungry again? Demon blood or just the kill? My blade is also restless, and I want to see Edward's strength. If my father gave him such power to help me, I need to know his limits."

Soul Eater stirred, and Sully felt control begin to slip. Closing his eyes, he waited to see if they would act as one—or if Soul Eater would take over completely. When he opened them again, he sensed Soul Eater wanted company. They would work together to feed their shared hunger.

Sully pulled a small mirror from his pocket and lifted it. One eye glowed yellow, the other blue. Since agreeing to the alliance, he had carried the mirror everywhere, afraid of losing himself completely—and betraying his destiny.

"Edward, let's go. We're hunting. Show me what Father gave you."

Sully smiled faintly, waiting for Edward to join him. Together they went searching for prey, Sully mindful that he had to choose carefully.

It didn't take long. Edward pointed toward a group huddled under a bridge. From a distance, Sully saw a barrel fire blazing, probably for warmth or light. He felt Soul Eater's eagerness, but he reminded himself of his mother's rules: they could only hunt rogues. A human life was forbidden unless necessary. For centuries his father's demon blood had tormented him, but this temptation pushed him to his limits.

Soul Eater whispered, *Brother. Your pain is torture. These are Balam's minions. Hunt them. Feed me. You won't break the rules. Imagine their warm blood in your throat. Kill them now.*

Sully's shoulders sagged, but his hands tightened. Moving closer, he saw Edward suspected nothing. Together they approached stealthily. The air grew cold, a mild breeze brushing the ground. Sully gripped his sword, motioning Edward to circle right while he took the left.

One demon noticed them and gasped. "It's the hunter."

The others turned, staring first at Sully, then at Edward. Sully raised his blade.

"Let's drink, brother," he said, though he would have preferred whiskey. Blood was the curse of his alliance.

He slipped into stance, sword arm ready, eyes on Edward. His brother seized one demon and tore into him without hesitation. That left three for Sully—and Soul Eater. He'd begged the entity to feed less on his soul since their last battle, but the wounds from that fight still hadn't healed. If demon blood would spare his soul further agony, Sully would endure the foul taste.

The three demons braced for him. Sully extended his free arm, beckoning. "Dance with me?"

The first flexed his muscles, cracking his neck with a grin. The second simply readied himself, while the third shifted nervously from foot to foot. Sully smirked.

"Planning to betray your king, demons?"

Soul Eater surged inside him, eager.

Now, brother?

"Now," Sully whispered.

As his gaze lifted, the demons saw his yellow eyes. Soul Eater was in control. The first demon recoiled in fear. "Shit—it's Soul Eater. Astaroth warned us about him. We're fucked."

Before the others could react, Sully's sword cut down in a single sweep. Three heads rolled. Blood dripped down the blade, and Sully lifted it to his lips and licked his sword. Once that was done, he began to drink the demons' blood, leaving only a shell of their former bodies until he said the words to send them back to Hell. Sully closed his eyes once more and regained his control while Soul Eater was satiated and retreated to his slumber.

***

Elias wandered the streets for hours until he encountered an angel. He recognized her instantly. Bowing his head, he said, "Jophiel, you're here."

Jophiel touched his head gently and smiled. She always came when he needed her. Elias glanced around to make sure the hunter's mother was safe. Seeing no threat, he poured out what he had learned, explaining that he needed to find the hunter.

"Prophet, I am here to help you," Jophiel said. "What is it you seek?"

"I need to find the hunter. The Second War is no longer a theory—it's coming, and he's at the center. You and Asmodeus must gain his favor equally to help him save the women and the world."

He spoke quickly, wary of hounds in the shadows or rogue demons—and perhaps even rogue angels. He waited for her answer. Instead, she reached into her blue robe and drew a small blade of gold and silver, bearing Heaven's emblem. She placed it in his hand. The blade hummed as his fingers closed around it.

"Is this what I think it is?" he asked.

Jophiel smiled. "Give this to Mick. She'll need it when she is cured. Michael gave it to me for my son, but you'll see him soon, prophet. I can't help much more, but know this: your purpose is to stay by the hunter's side. If you leave him, you risk the great plan. He has bound himself to both sides, but without one from each kingdom with him, he risks his soul—and all will be lost."

Elias's heart sank. The thought of the hunter losing his soul chilled him. He vowed to find Sully, deliver the blade, and never leave his side again—no matter the cost.

19

Mick convulsed several times under Katarina's watch. She was beginning to lose hope for her friend. Even though Lucifer and Asmodeus hadn't returned, Katarina knew she had to think of something fast. Calling for Balam was out of the question. Instead, she called on the one she thought was her best chance of saving Mick: Beelzebub.

Beelzebub was the demon most skilled in magic, manifestations, and manipulation. If anyone could manipulate Mick's mind enough to wake her, it would be him. When he appeared before her, Katarina noticed how his eyes never left Mick.

"I need you to manipulate her mind before Lucifer and Asmodeus return," she said. "Can you get her to wake up?"

Beelzebub licked his lips and sneered. Katarina stood firm, showing no fear. He raised his hand and slapped her across the face, leaving a red print.

"What the fuck was that for?" she demanded.

"Bitch, don't you know that woman reeks of Balam? And you want me to tamper with his work?"

Katarina clenched her fists and struck him hard. As he bent over in pain, she gripped his shoulders and drove her knee into his groin—once, then again, for good measure. Beelzebub crumpled to the ground, curled up and screaming. Katarina knelt, grabbed his chin, and hissed,

"I don't care if it was Balam or Lucifer who did this to Mick. I need you to wake her—fast."

Beelzebub nodded and moved to Mick's side. Katarina watched as he placed his hands on Mick's temples. Mick convulsed violently, foaming at the mouth, rejecting his power. He pushed harder, pouring more of himself into her, until Katarina feared Mick wouldn't survive at all. But she needed her awake. She had already decided—when Lucifer and Asmodeus left—that she and Mick would escape Hell and return to the hunter. Only by his side would they be safe.

Katarina studied Mick's face as her friend writhed under Beelzebub's power. Finally, Mick's eyes opened. Katarina breathed a sigh of relief—until she saw the emptiness in them. The glimmer was gone.

Beelzebub released her and stepped back. "Mistress Katarina, this is the best I could do. Balam put barriers in her mind. She can't communicate or remember—she's under his control completely. He'll know she's awake soon, and he'll come for you."

Katarina sighed and flicked her wrist, dismissing him. She took Mick's hands in her own and smiled faintly. "We're going to the hunter. Trust me, Mick. All I need is for you to trust me."

Before she could say anything else, Mick turned her eyes towards Katarina and spit in her face.

"I serve Balam. Not the hunter."

Katarina recoiled back in alarm, but her eyes fixed on Mick. She eyed her up and down and then noticed her eyes. Still the same shape and color but they were void of any signs of Mick. Scared, she grabbed onto Mick and shook her hard by the shoulders.

"Come back to me. Come back. I need you."

Mick's gaze drifted upward, cold. Katarina's chest tightened. Though she had once wanted the hunter all to herself, she had come to care for this woman. Their bond had begun out of necessity, then deepened through their shared love of the hunter. Now she knew she needed him to save her only friend.

She left the room, glancing back from the doorway. Mick's lips curled into an eerie smile, and she broke into uncontrollable laughter. Katarina clenched her fists at her sides, rage and fear burning toward Balam. Silently, she vowed to tear him apart piece by piece.

They all thought of her only as a seductress—but none of them, not even Lucifer, knew that the hunter had trained her in secret. She remembered his words – "*To be the hunter is always better than being the prey. Remember this to stay by my side forever.*"

***

Sully and Edward continued their search for the prophet. Edward grew restless and began talking. His questions stirred Sully's curiosity.

"Brother, remember when it was just you and me? Now that Father gave me this new body, what do you really think of my fighting?"

Sully chuckled at his brother's playfulness. Aside from having different mothers, they both shared Asmodeus's gifts for fighting—and lust.

"There were times I thought you were a noisy demon child," Sully said. "But now, Father has given you the transformation I need for my destiny. Still, I fear the path we're on is as dangerous as walking away from it. My circle of trust is small: you, the prophet, Soul Eater, Mick, and Katarina. But Edward...what if I walked away? I would forsake everything just to be normal."

He hoped Edward would understand that his birthright felt less like a gift and more like a burden. He missed the pure demon-hunting he once knew. Now, his dreams were filled with Soul Eater's past deeds, leaving sleep no longer peaceful. Each day, the pull between his duty and his longing for peace grew heavier.

Edward looked down and stayed silent. Though his father had transformed his body into that of a full-grown demon, Sully realized his mind was still that of a child. Once again, he felt the sting of abandonment he had carried all his life.

Edward finally looked up, and Sully's face softened. His eyes shifted yellow. Soul Eater was in control. Sully could only watch.

"Edward, Sully's soul is in pain," Soul Eater said. "His wound from Balam hasn't healed. Being separated from Mick and Katarina only makes it worse. If he breaks his oath, neither Heaven nor Hell can save him. Then my agreement takes effect—I'll devour his soul before returning to Lucifer. Will you save your brother? Will you bring him back?"

Edward hesitated. "What torment? Sully has always been in control. He never talks about pain. What changed?"

Soul Eater searched Sully's mind and returned with an answer. "When Balam attacked him, Sully was poisoned. He only recently became aware. The demon Katarina has the power to draw it out, but only she can. If not, the hunter will die—and everything that must happen will fail."

Edward frowned. "Who would want to live with poison in their body? That's too much for either kingdom to ask."

Soul Eater smiled. "You don't understand. If the torment continues, it will consume him. Balam designed it that way. The hunter is strong, but still mortal. Both Heaven and Hell swore to protect him—that was the pact. But Balam crafted a poison that drives him toward madness. If that happens, the world ends. The hunter must remain free. Each choice he makes serves both kingdoms. That's why Asmodeus fought so hard for his trust. But even now, he doesn't trust fully. There's more to his destiny than anyone admits. He seeks truth. And he needs us to help him."

Edward asked, "Does Sully know what you've just told me?"

Soul Eater laughed. "No. I've placed him in a deep slumber so I could be frank with you. As his brother, you must help him—no matter the cost. I ask you on his behalf. Help save the hunter. But you will need the prophet first."

$$20$$

Lucifer and Michael spoke for hours about how to help Mick. They came to an agreement, and Lucifer was confident that if they could save her, his demoness Katarina would remain at the hunter's side and soon bear his child. He knew he had to play the game to win. Deception was his nature, and if he could fool his brother, the more power he would hold. Defeating the rogue demons would only preserve his reign in Hell.

Asmodeus and Lucifer returned to Hell, Ramses keeping pace with their quick stride. Michael would be at Hell's gates with the hunter, Edward, and the prophet. The agreement between Lucifer and Michael was simple: the five of them could never part again for any reason. Michael agreed that the gates of Heaven would open for Katarina if she obeyed the hunter's every request. Her entrance to Heaven would depend on her obedience to him.

Lucifer knew he had to tell Asmodeus the truth, though he worried about his reaction.

"Asmodeus, my faithful demon. I made an agreement with Michael to save the woman. There is a price to pay—and it's yours. As your lord, I command your obedience once you hear what was decided. I am not asking your decision. I am informing you of it. Understood?"

Asmodeus was silent but nodded. Lucifer pressed on.

"You must release Edward and the hunter. Mick and the prophet may enter Hell's gates only if the hunter is with them. Katarina, Edward, and Mick may enter Heaven under the same condition. They must never be separated, or Mick cannot be saved. The hunter must share his bed with both women equally. Katarina must bear his child. That child will be ours—yours and mine. A hunter's child in Hell to protect us. All for saving Michael's daughter and keeping your son in line."

Asmodeus's eyes widened. Lucifer laid a hand on his shoulder and ch uckled. "It's brilliant. Michael suspects nothing of the surprises I've woven into this plan. Relax, demon. Let's go save my niece."

Ramses trotted up beside Lucifer, who rested a hand on the hound's head. Through him, Lucifer heard Cerebrus's thoughts. They were on their way to find the prophet and the hunter, but Cerebrus also reported the demons' schemes to usurp Lucifer's throne and shatter both kingdoms' balance. Lucifer clenched his fists. His plan had to succeed. He only hoped his deception would be enough for Michael to spare him if the truth came out.

Michael was already waiting at the gates. When the truce between kingdoms was forged, conditions had been written to allow entry from both sides if it was to protect the hunter. Using that guise, Lucifer made it possible to have Michael enter.

***

Katarina was preparing to depart when she turned around and faced Lucifer. Her heart pounded in fear but quieted when he raised his hand.

"Demoness, we left her in your care. Asmodeus is my witness. What have you done?"

She shut her eyes, arms at her sides, and whispered, "I summoned Beelzebub to bring her back, but he failed. Mick is different now. Even he couldn't save her. She belongs...to Balam."

Lucifer roared. Katarina's chest tightened—her life was worthless in his eyes. Then she saw him appear behind Lucifer: a golden figure with broad shoulders, long flowing hair, and a gleaming sword across his back. Not a demon.

Katarina lowered her head in submission and pointed toward the room where Mick lay. They entered, stepping carefully. Mick stared blankly, her laughter echoing. A deep voice spoke through her lips:

"Do you like my surprise, Asmodeus? You will be the downfall of your sons. Then Lucifer will have no choice but to bow to Astaroth and the others. Hell will be ours, and you will serve me."

Katarina rushed forward, trying to grasp Mick's hands—but claws slashed into her skin. She screamed and pulled back, blood clotting and burning on her arms.

Breaking the silence, she cried out, "I submit to you again, Lucifer. I recognize only you as my lord. Save my friend, and my eternal obedience is yours alone."

As she waited for his reply, the golden man stepped to her side. She froze, unsure what he meant to do, until he lifted her chin and studied her face. His features softened; he smiled.

He turned to Lucifer and said, "Brother, I agreed to help you. But this demon woman is more than she seems. Can't you see it?"

Katarina blinked in confusion. More than she seemed? She had always felt different, but...what was he implying? She turned to Lucifer, silently demanding an answer.

Before anyone could speak, she bolted. She left Hell at once, determined to find the hunter. Sully was her only chance to survive this chaos.

21

What felt like an eternity was just a matter of hours when Elias found Edward. The hunter was nowhere in sight. He saw Edward leaning against a lamppost and ran toward him. Out of breath, Elias began to tell him everything he had learned—only for Edward to raise his hand, stopping him.

"Prophet, breathe. My brother will be here soon. Soul Eater needed to feed again," he said in a dismayed tone.

Elias pressed on, ignoring Edward's words. "There will be a Second War. The hunter can no longer fight on his own. We need to stand by him through everything. Let me start from the beginning. You—just shut up and listen for once, Edward. Please. This is to protect the hunter. There's no time to waste."

Edward rolled his eyes, but Elias ignored it. He told him everything, from the attack to his meeting with Jophiel. As Elias paused, he noticed Edward was interested—though worry shadowed his face.

"What has you worried, friend?" Elias asked.

"You haven't mentioned anything about our father. Doesn't he play a part in this Second War that's coming?"

Elias sighed deeply. He hoped this detail would ease the hunter's brother. "Asmodeus is part of the pact, just like the archangel Jophiel. They will always be the hunter's birth family. The truce that ended the first war protects them. But the unknown rests on the hunter's choices and his free will. This war will be different. You and I can't protect him alone. Where is he? Can you summon Soul Eater?"

Edward just stared, and Elias's patience thinned. Transformation or not, Edward was still the demon child who had clung to the hunter for years. Elias took a breath, regaining calm. The longer he lingered in this world, the more he felt his Heavenly virtues slipping. He could not become like these men. He belonged back in Heaven. With a sigh, he laid a hand on Edward's shoulder and whispered a prayer.

Edward coughed. "I'll take you to him. Before you see him—Soul Eater was in control. He put Sully to sleep to talk to me. My brother said he wanted a normal life, to walk away. Soul Eater said his soul is in pain. He's the hunter—he's not supposed to feel pain. Can we help him?"

Elias smiled gently. "I was given the tools and knowledge to aid the hunter in his destiny. But he alone must choose. It's no coincidence he found Mick, Katarina, or even your transformation. It is destiny. Take me to him."

Edward led him through twisting alleyways. Elias stopped when he saw bodies of demons scattered on the ground. Each face was contorted and lifeless. A cold feeling came over him and the hair on his arms rose. Then he shifted his gaze to a man sitting against a wall. His head was hung low so he couldn't make out his features until he saw one of the tattoos light up the dark night. It was the tattoo given to him to acknowledge his identity. Elias ran to the man.

"Brother, brother! Can you hear me?"

The man raised his head and Elias looked straight into his eyes. He had to know which one of them was in control. Early on, he would mistake them until Sully made it clear: if both eyes were yellow, beware. Soul Eater was awake for his own purpose. And there it was—yellow eyes.

"Soul Eater, what happened to Sully? I have news, and we need somewhere safe to plan our next move."

"Prophet, you finally recognize me. The hunter sleeps so we can speak. You have news, and I have some for you. The balance shifts. Demons plot to change the world. You serve the King of Heaven, and I serve the King of Hell. But if the hunter abandons his birthright, there will be no king for either of us—and the world will end. Are you with me, prophet?"

Elias studied him, then asked, "Can you allow me to see Sully's soul? I won't go where I shouldn't, nor pry into your bond. I only want to know his state of mind."

Soul Eater nodded. Elias sat beside the hunter and closed his eyes, slowing his breath. His spirit slipped into Sully's mind.

Fragmented memories greeted him—glimpses of Sully's past since Eden. Elias pressed deeper, searching for the reason behind his suffering. Memories flooded him, and suffocation tightened in his chest. He couldn't risk dying here. He searched faster, harder. Finally, he found it: traces of demonic poison, and a strange hidden entity lurking, as if afraid of Soul Eater. Elias withdrew quickly, but resolved to uncover what it was.

Opening his eyes, Elias saw Sully—broken, despairing, without hope. He grasped his friend's hand. "Soul Eater?"

"I won't wake the hunter yet," Soul Eater replied. "We must finish our discussion. Is Edward here?"

"Yes. Come over, Edward. We need to return and talk. Soul Eater, can you keep Sully asleep until then?"

"Sully won't wake until we're done. The poison lingers in him—nothing else. His pain is intense. This hunter is handling his pain well enough but soon his power may fade. We need to go now."

With that said, the three of them returned to Sully's place to talk about next steps and to see if any of the books could help them.

****

Abaddon paced, her minions waiting for command. Frustrated by her failures, she knew she needed allies again—Astaroth and Balam. She couldn't face the hunter alone. But how? Then she remembered someone who could help. Margaret.

Her fists struck her thighs as she thought hard. *How can I do this and still break the hunter?*

At last, the idea struck. If she played submissive, she could regain favor with Astaroth and Balam—use them to lure the hunter to her. As long as she hid her true intentions, the plan might work. She recalled Balam boasting of the hounds. If they now obeyed Astaroth, she would focus on him. Astaroth was once an ally, now a formidable enemy. Winning his favor would be difficult—he never dropped his guard, especially around her. Then Margaret and her organization could handle the rest.

She turned to her minions, voice sharp. "Find Balam. Tell him I submit—on the condition I get to toy with the hunter, just to spite Lucifer. If he refuses, tell him I'll deliver the prophet, the demon seductress, and that bastard Edward in chains. A gift, if they let me back in their circle. All they'll need to do is destroy Lucifer."

One demon stepped forward, bowed, then turned to rally the others. Abaddon nodded, dismissing them.

With that handled, she reached for her phone and dialed a memorized number. "Margaret, it's me. Abaddon. The trap is set. Let's meet."

The reply came quiet, almost a whisper. "Come alone to the Lounge at the Venetian Hotel. Thirty minutes."

The line went dead.

22

Mick watched these fools make a fuss over her while at the same time panicking in their boots. She silently laughed at their audaciousness, but in her mind she only heard Balam's voice. She decided it was time to respond.

"Master, I am awake. These idiots are panicking on how to save me. What is your command?"

Her eyes darted from person to person in the room. They called her "Mick," but she had no recollection of anything except that she belonged to Balam and he was her master. A woman with black hair kept trying to hold her hand, while the others stood back just watching. Then she disappeared. A glowing man, different from the rest, stared at her in wonder. The other two were demons.

The voice answered her call. "Woman, they are not your friends. They may appear to care for you, but it is they who keep you trapped here. You belong to me and serve only me. Remember that. Find a way to come to me. I've given you special gifts before. You can only hear my voice. No one else's. Now come to me."

The voice was direct and commanding. She knew she had no choice but to obey. Now, how was she going to get out of here?

She watched them closely until something inside her snapped. Mick threw off the bedcovers and stood. A strange surge of power filled her. Confident she could escape these criminals and reach her master, she believed these people were holding her captive to harm her.

She closed her eyes, breathed deeply, then snapped them open. Instead of speaking, she walked straight up to the one Balam had described as Lucifer. He must have told her about him before she woke in this hellhole. Staring into his eyes, she raised her hand and slapped him hard across the face—once, then again. Two strikes.

Without hesitation, she shoved the others aside and stormed out. She knew how to find her master, and her journey began. Before she left the room, she heard one of them say, "Michael, she's not Mick anymore and she's strong. We need the hunter."

***

Katarina made it to Vegas as she heard rumors that the hunter was here with his brother. Edward. She knew she could trust him as much as she could trust the hunter. But where would they be? The desert was treacherous, though she knew demons who lived there. She only needed to make sure no one was following her.

While roaming the streets, she found a vendor selling shirts and assorted items. His eyes intrigued her. Katarina stopped and looked him over before saying a single word:

"Copernicus."

There was no meaning to the word itself, but only one demon in the world knew it as a code—Amaymon, the one she trusted most.

At once, he closed his stall, shooing away the customers. When they were alone, Katarina explained everything that had happened in Hell, how Mick—the hunter's woman—was in danger.

Amaymon kept glancing around nervously, not his usual behavior. Then he put two fingers to his mouth and whistled. Another demon appeared at his side, equally unsettled. *What the fuck was going on here?*

He motioned for her to follow, leading her into a dark alley. Katarina grew tired of these cat-and-mouse games.

"What's going on, Amaymon?"

"Demoness, you know I am fond of you," he said, touching her cheek.

"What do you want? I don't have time for your games."

"Oh, demoness, let me have a little fun with you. Just like old times. But that's not the point. Lucifer sent a messenger to his trusted demons. He knows what Astaroth and Balam are plotting. I am to ask you this question on his behalf: Are you loyal to him? Remember, I'll know if you lie. You know my special gift."

Katarina swallowed hard. She was loyal—but could she trust Amaymon? Teeth clenched, she chose to trust him. Worst case, she would die from his poisonous breath, and the hunter—or even Lucifer—might avenge her. She nodded.

"I am loyal to Lucifer, the true King of Hell. I am also bound to the hunter, who serves both kingdoms. I swear to Lucifer that he is my only master."

Amaymon stayed quiet—sending confirmation to Lucifer. It was their way of communicating, since Amaymon preferred to live among men.

Finally, he said, "Demoness, the path you've chosen is dangerous. Loyalty to Lucifer is one thing, but to be the hunter's woman is another. I see through you. Lucifer has replied. Do you want to hear it?"

Katarina tossed her black hair to one side, tilting her head. She let her eyes do the talking, coyly tempting him for information. Smiling, she nodded.

"Lucifer commands you to find the hunter and bring him back to Hell. He will need the prophet and Edward at his side. You are to tell him to invoke the Soul Eater and serve the master at once."

"Understood," she said.

Amaymon laughed. "Now, let's talk about our business. Isn't that why you came?"

His hand stroked her cheek, stroking softly and shifting away her hair to expose the side of her neck. His lips gently touched her neck, and he moved his mouth to hers while his hand slid up her skirt. Katarina knew she had to comply because she already confirmed her loyalty, and she would need information from him later.

***

Asmodeus was on his way to the tree where he always met Jophiel in secret. Though on different sides, they shared a bond beyond Sully. The tree itself symbolized their pact: giving up Sully to his adoptive parents if they ever needed to protect him together.

As he drew near, he saw Jophiel was already there. Alone.

He shifted his form into the one she most desired and stood before her. He loved Jophiel more than either kingdom would permit. For her alone filled his heart and mind.

"My love," he whispered.

Her smile told him he was the only one she held dear, even though he was the demon of lust. They had a son together, and they had agreed to the pact's terms. He could be with countless women, but she was his only one.

He reached for her lips—and suddenly their mouths met. He surrendered to her kiss for long minutes before pulling away. As much as he longed for her, Mick's situation demanded priority.

"Michael's daughter is under Balam's control," Asmodeus said. "We need our son to free her. Help me find him, Jophiel. Please."

Jophiel smiled, lifting her hand to reveal a strange weapon: a thin, small blade unlike any he had seen. He extended his finger close to it—without touching. The blade glowed red. He pulled back, and when her finger neared, it turned blue.

Asmodeus's eyes widened.

She laughed. "The blade changes color by kingdom. But once given to our son, it will merge into one, releasing new powers destined to keep him and his chosen companions safe from unworthy souls. With this blade, he can kill angels or demons who defy the kingdoms. He will be judge, jury, and executioner by his birthright."

Asmodeus placed his finger beside hers, both touching the blade. The colors merged, and as with Sully's sword once before, fire shot from its tip into the sky and down into the earth.

"It's ready," Jophiel said. "We need to find our son."

Asmodeus nodded, realizing again how much he loved this angel—even though such love was forbidden. Both kingdoms had granted them only one allowance: to birth the hunter.

<h1 style="text-align:center">23</h1>

Soul Eater was still in control, and as he spoke with Elias, he grew increasingly fond of the prophet. He began to understand why Elias had become a favorite of certain demons. Watching the prophet's behavior, he decided to ask pointed questions for the hunter's sake.

"Prophet, tell me something. You were sent to help the hunter. If the hunter goes astray and forsakes his birthright, what happens then? Do you know?"

Soul Eater was taking a chance on the response, but information was power—especially since he was Lucifer's servant, now allied with the hunter. He needed to know where loyalty truly lay.

Elias nodded and stayed silent for a few minutes. Soul Eater knew the signs—he was communicating with his kingdom, maybe even others.

Finally, Elias said, "Both kingdoms are in peril right now. Asmodeus and Jophiel are already on their way to us. We need to greet them and speak openly about the hunter. I beg you, do not wake the hunter until we talk with them first. Then we bring him in. All I can tell you is that we must prepare—and we need absolute loyalty from those the hunter can trust.

No exceptions. I also know the hell hounds are searching for the hunter. It's only a matter of time before everything comes full circle. The hunter needs us, and he is the one we protect."

Soul Eater listened carefully, but the mention of the hell hounds unsettled him. What was Cerebrus thinking? He had always been Lucifer's most loyal. Before Soul Eater could dwell on it, Asmodeus and Jophiel appeared.

Even after centuries in Lucifer's service, it was still strange to see a demon lord and an archangel standing side by side. But Soul Eater noticed how perfectly matched the hunter's parents were. At that moment, he realized he might need to ally with Michael, the archangel. Yet he was a soul eater—he feasted on the souls of demons, angels, and the forsaken. If he was to change, it was time to face Lucifer himself.

But first, he needed to hear what Asmodeus and Jophiel had to say. He knew his place compared to the hunter's parents.

"Lord Asmodeus, Angel Jophiel. You came for a reason. Please speak. Your servant, Soul Eater, eagerly awaits your orders."

Asmodeus chuckled. "Still Lucifer's sly servant—and my son's ally."

Jophiel lifted the blade destined for Sully. "This is for our son. It allows him to strike against demons or angels who no longer serve our purpose. It will guide him to discern who is bound to the pact between our kingdoms, and it will destroy those who oppose it. Before he accepts this blade, he must make peace with his path. His heart is broken—as his mother, I feel his pain. To guide him against what is coming, those who stand with our son must never abandon him. He needs both sides together to continue his path. Will you choose to stand by him?"

Soul Eater reached out and accepted the gift on Sully's behalf. Their bond had formed through an unholy alliance, but over time, Soul Eater had come to see the hunter as a brother in arms. He knew the torment Sully was enduring, and though it strained their connection, he remained loyal.

He remembered Lucifer's command: *Merge with the hunter, feast on his soul, and protect him at all costs. In return, I will give you your freedom. But you will be bound to the hunter for eternity.*

Soul Eater said, "We will stand by the hunter but from my sources, Mick is in danger and Katarina left Hell to find us. We need to return to Hell immediately."

***

Katarina wandered for hours after leaving Amaymon, lost in thought, until a voice broke through.

Demoness. Go to this address now.

The voice gave her a location in another part of Vegas. She diverted her course at once. The voice was familiar, though different. Then it struck her—it was Soul Eater. The hunter must be in trouble!

Moments later, on her way to the address, a hell hound blocked her path. She had rarely interacted with them in Hell and had never wronged one enough to be hunted. Locking eyes, she recognized her: Eve, the mother of all, one of Lucifer's favorites besides Cerebrus and Ramses.

Katarina tilted her head right, then left, testing for a reaction. Nothing. Eve simply sat, watching. Katarina even cleared her throat, but the hound remained silent. *What is going on here?*

"Greetings, Eve," she said. "Am I needed for something that required you to fetch me?"

If nothing else, Katarina was skilled at setting the tone. Lucifer himself had praised this gift—her voice, her allure. It was what made her the demon seductress. With it, she could bend others to her will.

The hound barked once, then growled. She sniffed the air and let out a loud howl. Katarina understood—this was either a command or a message.

"How can I serve you? I am loyal to Lucifer," she pressed.

The hound stood and circled her. Katarina's chest tightened. Was she prey now? Whispers said Lucifer no longer controlled the hounds. Fear pricked at her.

Eve finally sat again and locked eyes with her. Calm washed over Katarina. Kneeling, she cupped the hound's head and spoke silently, knowing hell hounds preferred nonverbal speech.

Eve, tell me what you need. I will help you.

The hound stared back, then the words filled her mind:*Since you remain loyal to Lucifer, King of Hell, I will tell you. We are ordered to capture the hunter and the prophet by Astaroth. But that is not the true goal. Lucifer wants us to protect the hunter and return him to Hell. He is needed there. Ramses is with the king now. The hunter must return. Bring me to him—you are already heading there.*

Katarina blinked. The hound knew more than she let on. Eve spoke in riddles, but Katarina realized she would gain nothing more from her. She motioned for the hound to follow.

24

Mick was still struggling as Lucifer called demons to restrain her. Seeing how Asmodeus and Katarina had both left, he was determined to keep her safe at all costs. He decided to use this time to talk with Michael about their plan and how to utilize the hunter in this mess. Deep down, he had always wanted the hunter fully on his side, and deception was his middle name. Lucifer just wondered if he could succeed for once against the kingdom of Heaven.

"Michael, we need to talk. It's just you and me, brother."

Michael agreed but said nothing. Lucifer always knew his brother was guarded and righteous, but at this moment, Michael was in his kingdom. His kingdom. His rules. And Lucifer wasn't about to let this opportunity slip away. He laughed.

"Dear brother, fate is a bitch. You are a guardian angel, the sword of Heaven, and yet you are in Hell with me. I promised I wouldn't hurt my niece, but now neither you nor I can control her. Have you thought how we are going to break her free from Balam's grasp?"

Michael answered, "First, we talk about these factions in your kingdom, brother. The ones who want to overthrow you or start a Second War—as if the First War wasn't enough. Tell me, how do you want to talk about that?"

Lucifer shifted uneasily. He never understood why, as a fallen angel, he still grew uncomfortable around Michael. Maybe it was his presence, maybe his power—or his arrogant righteousness. Whatever it was, it was enough for Lucifer to hate him. But as he glanced at Mick, his cold heart softened. She looked like a pixie with her short dark hair and small face. He didn't see Michael in her, but someone else he couldn't quite place. That answer would come later. For now, he had to placate his brother.

"Mick is more important than anything you mentioned. She needs to be with the hunter. She is your daughter. I'll deal with those factions myself, and as ruler of this kingdom, I have no plans for a Second War. The First was lesson enough after I was thrown from Heaven. From Soul Eater's reports, the hunter is struggling with his commitment. We either ally together or let the two kingdoms end the truce. Either way, I'll get what I want in the end—either all mortals' souls, or the truce. Choice is yours, brother."

Michael swung his fist, landing a blow to Lucifer's cheekbone. Lucifer took it in stride—this time, he wasn't going to lose. Grinding his teeth, he stepped back, blocking Michael from another strike, then hit him in return, savoring the moment as the angel fell to the ground.

Knowing the rules had already been broken for Michael to even be in Hell, Lucifer shouted, "ENOUGH! We need to work together and bring the hunter here. He's the only one who can set my niece free. Help me—or I will banish you from Hell this minute! And if Mick survives or not, you'll have to live with it, brother."

Michael's fury was obvious, but they were still brothers—and Lucifer was still the king of deception. Their feud would always remain, regardless of any temporary truces. Family was family, and those bonds never broke.

Michael relented. "We will work together to save Mick. But if your factions start a Second War, every demon you command will die by my sword. That is my promise to you, brother."

Before they could continue, Mick broke free of her restraints and ran at them both. Michael looked devastated by his daughter's state, and Lucifer no better. He had already called Ramses, who gently pushed Mick back and held her firm with his weight.

"Lucifer, brother," Michael said. "If you want to be my brother, I will help you save my daughter. But if you go against me, I will use Heaven's Justice to right the wrong and punish your kingdom. Agree or not, brother."

Lucifer was trapped.

"I agree."

***

It's been forty-five minutes since she arrived, and Margaret still hadn't shown. Abaddon had already downed three shots, and no one else had come in except a couple, who left quickly. Finally, the doors opened, and two large men wheeled in a chair. The woman in it—Margaret.

The chair stopped in front of her. One man stood behind in a defensive position, ready to strike on command. The other shifted to Margaret's side and offered his hand. With grace, she rose from the chair and smiled.

Abaddon's eyes widened.

"I heard the hunter caused your paralysis. How can you stand now?"

Margaret only laughed. The two men stood silent and nodded. Abaddon wasn't sure what to make of it.

"The hunter will pay for what he did to me, I promise you that. I survived, but only with technology. I don't even feel human anymore. And you, a demon, are no better than me—so wipe that smug smile off your face."

Abaddon grew uneasy, but she knew Margaret was her last hope to get back into favor with the others and bring the hunter down. She swallowed her pride and reached out a hand.

"Hear me out. Then tell me if you can help."

She paused, waiting. Instead of Margaret, one of the bodyguards spoke.

"Tell our mistress your plan. If she likes it, one of us will stay by your side to help you. If not, we'll end you here and now."

Abaddon had no choice but to bite her tongue. This wasn't their agreement. Fury simmered, but she knew she had to play along.

"Margaret, don't mess around. You and I want the same thing—just with different methods. Astaroth released the hell hounds, Lucifer's most trusted. They no longer obey him. I need just one to drag the hunter to me. I have a way to subdue him and make his demon brother suffer. Once the hunter falls, Edward will be consumed by the others. The hunter will obey me, because thanks to Balam's touch, his woman is already under his control. He'll do anything to save her. He won't submit to Balam or Astaroth—Soul Eater won't allow it. But he'll submit to me. I just need the hound to bring him. It's foolproof. If you give me your man as promised, you must stay out of my way. When I'm done, I'll turn the hunter over to your organization. He won't serve Lucifer—if we join forces."

Margaret smiled and glanced at her bodyguard. Abaddon braced for a trick, anger boiling, but kept her composure.

Margaret touched her hand and said sweetly, "We can bring you a hound. Our technology has advanced to control both sides. Don't underestimate us. I will give you Bruce—my fiercest, most loyal guard. He'll help bring the hunter to you. As for his brother, Bruce has instructions from our organization to deal with that demon child. Asmodeus will do anything to protect him and will have to agree to my terms. Take Bruce now and go. Working with demons makes me sick."

With a flick of her wrist, the second bodyguard wheeled her away, leaving Abaddon alone with Bruce.

He extended his hand. She shook it, silent.

"Let's go. We have a lead." He touched his earpiece and started walking. Abaddon followed.

25

S oul Eater was determined to wrap things up and let Sully awaken. They needed to go to Hell, and he wanted the hunter to see his parents united. The pain Soul Eater felt from Sully was too intense; in fact, it prevented him from feasting on the hunter's soul, and he now relied on demons' blood to survive. He looked at their party and began thinking about how he was going to get them into Hell. He had no choice but to contact Lucifer.

One thing the other side never understood was Lucifer's name preference. He always went by several names, but he preferred Lord Lucifer—or just Lucifer. Satan was not a favorite of his.

"I need to contact Lord Lucifer. As his servant, I need to request permission to bring the other kingdom's servants with us to Hell. Archangel Jophiel, will you be joining us, or will you leave it to your *husband* to handle things?"

Soul Eater knew the word "husband" would make things clear for everyone as to their real relationship, and he secretly hoped the hunter would understand his intent when he awoke. He needed the hunter to feel secure and get his wild emotions under control, because the more tortured and insecure he became, the less Soul Eater could feast on his soul—and that was what bound them together.

Jophiel smiled. "I will return to Heaven. My task here is done, but I need a moment alone with Asmodeus. He needs to understand a few things about the blade to teach Sully."

Soul Eater motioned for them to step into another room to talk. While they waited, he asked the prophet to gather the most important books they would need and secure them. Then he asked Edward to prepare the weapons and anything else—elixirs included—that might help them. Soul Eater knew they would not be returning, and he planned to ask Jophiel to gather the remaining books to keep them safe for the hunter.

Minutes later, Jophiel and Asmodeus returned. Soul Eater noticed the worry etched on their faces, and ever since bonding with Sully, he had grown to care about these two. He understood, over time, why they had been chosen by both kings to create the hunter.

He clasped their hands in his and said, "Though I am not truly your son, I know what he feels. He agreed to his destiny to honor you both, but deep down, he isn't sure he wants this. His love for the world is pure. He grew up hunting demons, freeing the world from them—but a son loves his mother first and foremost. I believe he will come back from this torment stronger than ever, though much depends on the poison in his system. Archangel Jophiel, I ask that you keep the books safe for us when we return. Asmodeus, you must protect both sons and your service to Lord Lucifer. Betrayal will force your son to kill you—with my help. Loyalty above all is required. I will send word to Lord Lucifer that only the prophet seeks permission to return to Hell. I sense that Mick is in need, and Katarina must accompany us."

Before they could leave, the figure of a woman and a hell hound appeared before them. Soul Eater recognized the pair at once.

Katarina and hellhound Eve.

***

Katarina looked at the group as the hunter started to approach them. She couldn't reveal what she and Eve had communicated about earlier. Eve snarled, and Katarina raised her hand as though commanding the hound. Asmodeus approached with Jophiel at his side. Even though Katarina hadn't interacted much with angels, she saw immediately why the hunter was so protective of his mother.

"This is Eve," she said. "One of Lucifer's favorite hell hounds. We need to talk."

Whispers rippled through the room until Soul Eater spoke. "Eve is Lucifer's favorite, next to Cerebrus, Ramses, and Raphael. But it's unusual that she's calm and not attacking. Something is wrong here. Katarina, what's going on? We already know some pieces, but maybe you know more?"

Katarina smiled and sauntered over to Soul Eater. Lightly touching his arm, she spoke in a coy voice. "Lucifer needs us back in Hell. Eve is to remain at the hunter's side. Mick's life is in danger if she stays under Balam's control. The hunter needs her—and he needs me. Two pretty birds. One hunter. You do the math. Asmodeus—you know I'm right. I was there, and so were you, when Mick woke up like a crazy bitch."

The others didn't move—Eve blocked their path. Katarina turned back to the hound and knelt once again. Eve seemed to hold answers they needed. As before, she cupped the hound's face and locked eyes, speaking silently the way hell hounds communicated. She asked if Eve could tell her what to do.

Lucifer and the "golden man" were in Hell, the hunter and his family were here with her and a hound. It was bizarre, but stranger things existed in this fucked-up world.

Katarina rose and said, "Time to go. Those coming with me to Hell—let's go. We need to save Mick. Those staying, like the angel—take care."

Soul Eater only shrugged. Katarina knew they had one chance to save Mick and tell the hunter what was happening—but first, they needed to stand before Lucifer and the golden man.

26

Balam slammed his fist into one of the demons who had brought word that the hunter had reunited with Asmodeus and an angel. The demon didn't know which angel, but Balam guessed it was his mother. That was the only angel Asmodeus had ever been seen with other than Michael. He realized Asmodeus was playing them. Turning to Astaroth, he whispered,

"I will break the girl. She's already under my control, but I can still have her turn on the hunter. That will break them both. Then let's see what the hunter can do."

Astaroth smiled and clasped his hands together. "Balam, I wonder if it's time to bring Abaddon back. I heard rumors that she met a woman in a wheelchair who is also interested in controlling the hunter. Perhaps we should partner with her as well. Our numbers would be bigger to overthrow Lucifer, and if we are strong enough, we can force a Second War. What do you think?"

"A Second War? That would destroy both kingdoms. Astaroth, do you realize if we start this war, the world will end? The hunter will be nothing more than a slave. Without the world of man, we won't be able to have cambions or anything else. Are you sure about this? I thought we wanted to use the hunter, not turn him into a slave."

Before he could react, Astaroth's fist smashed into the side of his face. As Balam staggered back, he realized he, too, was being deceived—just as Astaroth intended to deceive Abaddon. *Damn demon.* Shaking off the impact, Balam steadied himself. Astaroth was insane.

"Are you out of your fucking mind?" Balam growled.

Astaroth swung again, but Balam dodged, expecting it.

"Don't test me, Balam. Remember who is superior among us."

Balam lowered his head and gritted his teeth. He needed to get the woman away from Hell to lure the hunter into their trap. She was no use to him while she remained with Lucifer. With his head still bowed, he sent a message to the woman to rise and come directly to him. Then he sent another—this one to Abaddon.

Abaddon. It's time. We need to move up our plan to destroy Astaroth. His idea of a Second War will destroy everything we've worked for. He must be removed before we can destroy Lucifer. Meet me in an hour. Usual place."

***

In Hell, Mick sat upright and looked around. The demon's voice was in her head again. Clutching her ears, she screamed. When she finished, she looked into Lucifer's eyes. Her brown eyes darted, clouded with pain as a headache seized her.

Michael rushed to her side, Lucifer trailing behind. She felt a familiar hand on her shoulder, but it angered her. Mick shoved it away and lashed out at both of them. She was instructed to return to Balam—the voice that controlled her every thought and movement. He was inside her head.

She opened her eyes wide and stared at Michael. For a moment she felt a flicker of familiarity. Reaching for his hand, she smiled. But once their hands touched, the smile twisted vicious.

"You will die by my hand, Father. The hunter will be bound to me. He will suffer, and the hounds will feast on what's left after Balam breaks him. He will no longer serve either kingdom."

Fear flashed in Michael's eyes, but Mick didn't give them a chance to answer. She leapt from the bed, slashed her nails across Lucifer's face, struck Michael with her other hand, and vanished.

Wandering the tunnels of Hell, she encountered several demons. She was no longer afraid of them. They didn't attempt to capture her this time. She remembered enough of her old self to know who she was—but Balam's power gave her a thrill she had never felt before. No longer the timid woman who had once clung to the hunter, Mick now relished the cold strength flowing through her veins. Balam's whispers filled her mind, urging her, and she listened. She had no choice. Even when she thought of the hunter, warm memories clashing with her new self, sharp pains tore through her abdomen and her head until she submitted again.

She walked past one demon who simply stood and watched her. When she came close, she grabbed him by the throat, squeezing hard. Her voice rang out—but it was Balam's.

"Meet my new toy, demon brother. She is strong, but she obeys me. Follow her, for she will come to me. The hunter will soon be ours."

She released the demon and continued walking. Others fell in line behind her, following. Periodically, she tried to resist Balam by thinking of the hunter in happier times. Each time, pain ripped through her until she surrendered again.

In one brief, pain-free moment, she sent a message to her father. It was short because she didn't want to have another sharp pain. All she could say was "*Save the hunter to save me. Help me.*"

Deep down, Mick hoped it was enough for her father to understand. After all, her father was the infamous archangel Michael.

***

Margaret was an impatient woman, so she secretly arranged for Abaddon to be followed. Her men had just reported in: Abaddon was meeting with others, talking with Bruce about capturing the hunter. But they noticed something troubling—she kept her distance from Bruce, the very bodyguard Margaret had given her. That infuriated Margaret. If the demon bitch didn't trust her, how was Bruce supposed to provide the location of Hell's gates?

She forced herself calm as she listened, then snapped her orders. "Listen. Increase the guard by four men. Add a woman who can get close to that demon bitch. Use the one Asmodeus sent us long ago—we call him Malcolm, but to the demons he is Ipes. They think we don't know he's their spy, but we do. We keep him only to control their little power game. Make sure you install a tracker on his phone. I want Hell's location. Nothing else matters. I'll inform my father and uncle and have them mobilize forces when the time comes."

She hung up and turned to the bodyguard beside her. "Prepare the needles for the hell hounds. I want at least five under our control."

"Yes, madam. I'll make the arrangements. Another guard will relieve me to protect you."

Margaret watched him use his earpiece, then move behind her wheelchair as if to push her elsewhere. But they didn't move. Instead, she felt a hard blow to the back of her head. The world went dark.

When she came to, she was surrounded by Astaroth and Balam. Her three trusted bodyguards stood at their side. She scanned quickly. Malcolm was missing.

Had she been wrong about him—or had she fallen right into their trap?

***

In Hell, Mick sat upright and looked around. The demon's voice was in her head again. Clutching her ears, she screamed. When she finished, she looked into Lucifer's eyes. Her brown eyes darted, clouded with pain as a headache seized her.

Michael rushed to her side, Lucifer trailing behind. She felt a familiar hand on her shoulder, but it angered her. Mick shoved it away and lashed out at both of them. She was instructed to return to Balam—the voice that controlled her every thought and movement. He was inside her head.

She opened her eyes wide and stared at Michael. For a moment she felt a flicker of familiarity. Reaching for his hand, she smiled. But once their hands touched, the smile twisted vicious.

"You will die by my hand, Father. The hunter will be bound to me. He will suffer, and the hounds will feast on what's left after Balam breaks him. He will no longer serve either kingdom."

Fear flashed in Michael's eyes, but Mick didn't give them a chance to answer. She leapt from the bed, slashed her nails across Lucifer's face, struck Michael with her other hand, and vanished.

Wandering the tunnels of Hell, she encountered several demons. She was no longer afraid of them. They didn't attempt to capture her this time. She remembered enough of her old self to know who she was—but Balam's power gave her a thrill she had never felt before. No longer the timid woman who had once clung to the hunter, Mick now relished the cold strength flowing through her veins. Balam's whispers filled her mind, urging her, and she listened. She had no choice. Even when she thought of the hunter, warm memories clashing with her new self, sharp pains tore through her abdomen and her head until she submitted again.

She walked past one demon who simply stood and watched her. When she came close, she grabbed him by the throat, squeezing hard. Her voice rang out—but it was Balam's.

"Meet my new toy, demon brother. She is strong, but she obeys me. Follow her, for she will come to me. The hunter will soon be ours."

She released the demon and continued walking. Others fell in line behind her, following. Periodically, she tried to resist Balam by thinking of the hunter in happier times. Each time, pain ripped through her until she surrendered again.

In one brief, pain-free moment, she sent a message to her father. It was short because she didn't want to have another sharp pain. All she could say was *"Save the hunter to save me. Help me."*

Deep down, Mick hoped it was enough for her father to understand. After all, her father was the infamous archangel Michael.

***

Margaret was an impatient woman, so she secretly arranged for Abaddon to be followed. Her men had just reported in: Abaddon was meeting with others, talking with Bruce about capturing the hunter. But they noticed something troubling—she kept her distance from Bruce, the very bodyguard Margaret had given her. That infuriated Margaret. If the demon bitch didn't trust her, how was Bruce supposed to provide the location of Hell's gates?

She forced herself calm as she listened, then snapped her orders.

"Listen. Increase the guard by four men. Add a woman who can get close to that demon bitch. Use the one Asmodeus sent us long ago—we call him

Malcolm, but to the demons he is Ipes. They think we don't know he's their spy, but we do. We keep him only to control their little power game. Make sure you install a tracker on his phone. I want Hell's location. Nothing else matters. I'll inform my father and uncle and have them mobilize forces when the time comes."

She hung up and turned to the bodyguard beside her. "Prepare the needles for the hell hounds. I want at least five under our control."

"Yes, madam. I'll make the arrangements. Another guard will relieve me to protect you."

Margaret watched him use his earpiece, then move behind her wheelchair as if to push her elsewhere. But they didn't move. Instead, she felt a hard blow to the back of her head. The world went dark.

When she came to, she was surrounded by Astaroth and Balam. Her three trusted bodyguards stood at their side. She scanned quickly. Malcolm was missing.

Had she been wrong about him—or had she fallen right into their trap?

27

Cerebrus and Raphael reunited when they realized that Eve was missing. As leader, Cerebrus took it upon himself to be in charge. He convinced Raphael to merge into one hound so that the two of them would not be separated. Once he learned that Eve was with the demoness Katarina, he decided it was time to find the hunter. Lord Lucifer was on his own, and his demons were turning against him. The only way to save his master was to play along with these demons.

Luckily, his master and Asmodeus knew their plans all along. Hell hounds only served Lucifer, so convincing everyone that Lucifer had lost control of Hell's domain meant pretending the hounds were no longer bound to him. Using their silent form of communication, Cerebrus reached out to Eve.

Tell me where you are. We need the hunter. You must get the hunter to follow our control.

Eve responded. With her location now known, Cerebrus and Raphael both howled and ran toward the hunter. As they raced through the streets of Vegas, they found numerous souls to bring back to their master. Cerebrus made note of them, knowing souls delivered to Lord Lucifer would strengthen his rule—and that was what he needed most now. With murmurs of Astaroth planning a Second War and a takeover of Hell, the hounds had to gather as many souls as possible for their master.

Cerebrus sniffed the air and caught the scents: the hunter and the prophet, together. Then he sniffed again: Eve. Asmodeus. And an angel. He howled loudly to announce his presence. Before he could take another step, Eve greeted him and merged. Now they were three heads on one body. Their dark brown fur thickened, and around their necks gleamed three ornate collars, marking their importance to Lord Lucifer. Their combined form was larger than the separated bodies, their strength magnified—enough to destroy anyone who stood in their way.

Still in charge, Cerebrus led. He shoved open the door, and before anyone could object, all three hounds let out one unified howl that was louder than ever. They stood at attention and maintained control of the situation.

It was Asmodeus who came towards them first. He bent down and offered his hand for Cerebrus to acknowledge. The two exchanged a knowing look and Cerebrus realized that Asmodeus had not betrayed his master. It was getting harder to tell which demons went to Astaroth's side and which ones remained loyal to Lord Lucifer.

Cerebrus howled once more as if to direct Asmodeus and his group to follow. Instead of them responding, the hunter approached. He studied the hunter again and decided to communicate through his mind.

"Hunter. I am Cerebrus, the alpha of all hell hounds. We serve our true master, Lord Lucifer.

The hunter laughed. "It is I, Soul Eater, who commands the hunter's body now. Give me the order, and it shall be obeyed."

Cerebrus peered closer, then saw it—the yellow eyes. It truly was Soul Eater.

Soul Eater. We must bring the hunter to the gates of Hell. He must choose carefully which side he serves. The winds of fate blow toward Astaroth, but the choice is his. His woman is already under Balam's control. He must either reaffirm his oath or break it. Lord Lucifer knows he is torn, and I suspect the prophet knows as well. Another hound has been set on the hunter's trail—one that no longer obeys us. If that hound reaches him, it will set the stage for the Second War. Everyone speaks of it. It is time to go, but the angel must leave. Her scent is hard for any hound to resist.

Soul Eater nodded, relaying the message to the group. Katarina stepped forward. "Looks like Eve is reunited. Are we ready to go back and save Mick?"

Cerebrus howled in affirmation.

They set off for the gates of Hell—except Jophiel, who stayed behind. Only Eve turned her head to show respect to the hunter's mother. Cerebrus pressed forward, leading them, until a group of demons blocked their path.

"Hand over the hunter!" one shouted. "Astaroth is waiting."

Drool dripped from Cerebrus's jaws as he saw the hunter step forward, Edward and the prophet close behind. Asmodeus and Katarina veered left, circling the demons. A battle was about to erupt. Then Cerebrus noticed the hunter's eyes shift—Soul Eater and Sully were now united.

Word had spread through Hell of the countless battles the hunter had fought, and every hound wanted to witness it. The demons knew the hell hounds were intelligent and loyal to Lord Lucifer, able to understand everything around them. Nothing escaped Cerebrus's notice.

He stood back to watch. Raphael and Eve obeyed his command, remaining silent. He studied the hunter's stance—feet steady, sword raised. Cerebrus was impressed by his agility and swordsmanship. The hunter spun the blade in a circle above his head, then brought it down hard and fast, cleaving the first demon. Without pause, he swung again, killing the others.

Then Cerebrus saw it—both eyes glowing yellow, tattoos blazing. The hunter drank the demons' blood and licked the blade clean.

Now Cerebrus understood why he was the chosen one. But as he watched closely, he noticed the hunter favored his side more than he should. Was he injured? How would Lord Lucifer react? Cerebrus sent a message to his master, warning him of the injury. To keep Astaroth at bay, he also sent another message:

We hounds have the hunter. We also have the demoness, the prophet, and Asmodeus's son Edward. We await your command.

Astaroth's reply came swift:*I command all hounds to destroy the demons still loyal to Lucifer. Bring me the hunter and the prophet. Send one hound to capture the prophet. I want them bowing before me within three hours.*

Cerebrus howled. It had begun. The battle among demons was starting, and he knew they had to return to Lucifer's side immediately. Fortunately, Asmodeus was aware of the plan and urged them onward.

28

Balam had been waiting for Mick while listening to the orders Astaroth was giving. Time was running out. He and Abaddon had an agreement to take down Astaroth before going after Lucifer. Astaroth's vengeful nature, his obsession with starting a Second War, was throwing everything into chaos. This war wasn't demon against demon. It was shaping into a full-blown replica of the First War—angels against demons, kingdom against kingdom.

Even though Balam no longer cared for the pact, a Second War could not happen. It would mean complete annihilation of everything, including demons. There had to be a way to use Mick to stop this and gain control over the hunter.

He had already uncovered the secrets hidden in Mick's mind. He wondered if she even knew she carried them. He decided he would have to test her. While waiting for her to arrive, he tried to understand what Astaroth was after.

Astaroth must have sensed his curiosity. His features softened slightly, but his caution remained.

"We will win once we control the hunter," Astaroth sneered. "Haven't you heard the rumors? His will is weakening. The foolish hunter doubts himself. Ever since we poisoned him, his willpower has been fading. Soon, he will feel so alone and isolated that even his precious brother Edward won't be able to pull him back."

Balam frowned. "I still don't see why the war is necessary. If the hunter favors one side, the pact is broken. We could overthrow Lucifer without it. No angel or demon loyal to both kingdoms would stop us."

Astaroth burst into laughter. "Balam, you're cunning, yes. Devious, yes. But you are also the biggest dumb fuck I've ever met. When the three of us are in control, we will rule both kingdoms. I want to rule Heaven and drive out the angels. I want them all to fall so their king is left with nothing but an empty throne."

Anger flared in Balam's chest. This was not the plan he and Abaddon had agreed upon. Now he saw it—Astaroth was planning to deceive them all. He wouldn't let him succeed. Conquering Heaven and annihilating the world would end demons, not just angels. He needed to tell Abaddon what secrets lay in Mick's mind. Those secrets were a ticking time bomb waiting to explode.

Before Balam could do anything, Mick appeared in front of him. She lowered herself in submission and in a meek voice, she said, "Master."

***

Lucifer paced the hall, waiting for something to happen. For the first time since the First War, he felt abandoned. He had just begun to get used to having his niece nearby, and it was a strange thing to feel family ties again. He quickly shook it off. He was the King of Hell, not some sentimental fool.

He had always known he wasn't favored by God, his father, or his brothers. But as he paced, his eyes drifted toward Michael—the archangel. His enemy. His family.

"Brother," Lucifer said, "what secrets did you place in Mick's mind? Balam has already seen them. If you let them take over Hell and destroy my kingdom, you leave me no choice but to destroy you."

He had hoped the words would strike a chord, but Michael's expression revealed nothing—no anger, no sadness. Lucifer studied him. He had never realized how similar they looked, aside from hair and eyes. Michael's sword glowed with heavenly light, strapped across his back. Lucifer wondered—if he had never fallen, would he have a sword like that? Would he have fought by his brother's side? Wishful thinking. He was the King of Hell. Nothing would change that.

Michael's silence gnawed at him. He wanted answers. Finally, Michael spoke.

"I gave Mick the maps to the gates. Not only that—she carries the true knowledge of the tree, of man, and of us. That knowledge was meant to protect the hunter, but now that Balam knows it, it will be used against us. My deepest shame is that I failed to protect her."

Michael never looked at him as he spoke. Lucifer felt unease stir in his chest. Was he becoming too soft?

"Ramses, come here."

The hound padded forward and sat obediently.

"Bring me three fresh souls. I am in the mood for torture."

Lucifer forced his emotions down. He was King of Hell.

Michael tried to stop him. "Lucifer, do you ever regret falling from Heaven—or making peace with me?"

Lucifer sneered. "I will always be the fallen angel. I have no regrets."

But even as he said it, a small spark of regret lingered in his heart, unspoken. He shoved it down. He didn't even know where he would begin if he tried to explain it.

Michael broke the silence. "The location of Heaven's gates is vital to the hunter's destiny. He must be able to pass freely between both kingdoms. The gates never open for the fallen—but with the key, he will have access. The key also serves another purpose. It unlocks a book that contains all of Heaven's secrets. You saw that book once, before you fell. And Mick—she is the embodiment of Eve. Did you know that, brother?"

Lucifer spun, eyes wide. Eve. The first woman. When he had first seen her, he had been infatuated, so much so that he named his hound after her. His fists clenched, his tongue pressed hard against his teeth. He knew then that he had to save his niece. But the passion he once felt for Eve was gone. His heart was consumed now by evil, by longing, by power.

"We will rescue her and bring her back to the hunter," Lucifer said. "Neither kingdom can fall, but mine will rule over man. That is man's destiny. They will be loyal to me."

He was adamant that his kingdom would rule humanity, but he acknowledged the pact's importance and the truce it upheld. He hoped Michael understood his true nature and would leave him be. But he knew better—Michael would always try to drag him back to Heaven, always urge him toward forgiveness.

Lucifer swore it would never happen.

29

It was an arduous journey, and with Sully fully awakened, Asmodeus took this time to explain things to his son. Edward helped Sully come to terms with the current events, especially those concerning Mick. But there was one thing Asmodeus hadn't accounted for—the blade Jophiel had given for their son.

He studied the weapon, noting the intricate symbols representing both Heaven and Hell. Looking closer, he turned to Sully's body. The symbols matched. And then he saw it—the one in the middle of the blade. Sully's signature marking, the one bestowed upon him by Asmodeus and Jophiel.

This special marking was unique to them as a sign of their union. A circle of geometric and arcane symbols represented his power, while a flaming gold sword tied to it in a subtle way, symbolizing their bond. The blade was meant for their son.

Asmodeus felt a sharp longing pain and placed a closed fist over his heart. He knelt on one knee.

"Son. I present this blade from your mother and me. You accepted your destiny, and you should know that if you choose to walk away, we will stand by you. But if you walk away, you will lose yourself completely. Your path is yours to take."

He paused, looking up at his son—the hunter. Sully stood over six feet tall, dark hair touched with gold highlights that appeared when he accepted his true sword. His muscular build had remained unchanged since his destiny began. But Asmodeus noticed something: his son's eyes were rarely blue anymore. More often, they were yellow—or a mix of blue and yellow. Soul Eater was taking control more frequently. That meant Sully was hurting in ways even his father couldn't understand.

He remembered Jophiel's words: their son needed acceptance from both sides.

"The group you've chosen—Mick, Katarina, Edward, the prophet—they are part of your destiny. Mick's soul and freedom hang in Balam's grasp. You and Soul Eater are one, regardless of the color of your eyes. Your despair comes from the poison in you. Without it, you wouldn't suffer as you do. Do you understand, Sully?"

Sully raked his fingers through his hair and lowered his head. Asmodeus watched him closely, listening to his breathing. When Sully raised his head again, both eyes glowed yellow.

In a deep voice, Soul Eater spoke: "The poison is spreading. I feel his pain. His torment is overwhelming him. If it seeps further, it will trigger something unimaginable. The prophet knows one version, and others may know another. The truth is this body is the trigger to the Second War. If the hunter walks away, his soul triggers war on both sides. Lucifer can tell you more. To control the poison, the hunter must drink the blood of his father and his mother. Not much—just enough to purge the poison. But the blood must come from the heart. Lucifer can explain further. We must go now, while I can still control his movements."

Asmodeus listened, his body trembling. Too much was happening at once: Astaroth's rebellion, Balam's control over Mick, demons hunting the prophet, his son's poisoning, and his own plans with Lucifer to keep everything balanced—even if it meant sacrificing himself for Sully. He would do it. He had promised Jophiel.

"We return to Hell now. Let's go. Edward, help your brother if needed but follow any instructions that come from Soul Eater. He is the one we follow until your brother regains control."

Asmodeus led the way with Katarina and the prophet next to him. He wanted to understand the prophet more to see why his son valued their friendship so much. Even though he sent Edward to him as a child, his two sons didn't click at first. But Sully had always told him that there was something about the prophet that made him feel comfortable with who he was.

"Prophet, what do you know about the Second War and what's coming?"

The prophet laughed and placed a hand on Asmodeus's shoulder. For a moment, warmth spread through him. Turning to look, Asmodeus noticed a faint light surrounding the man.

"I am Elias, the prophet who serves. My orders are to protect the hunter. What I know of the Second War is limited—it is the final battle between the kingdoms. Whoever wins will control both realms, and the world will be doomed. Mick, Michael's daughter, is essential to both sides. Like the hunter, she belongs to both. Their future depends on him saving her. And don't forget the hounds. There is more to them than we understand. Perhaps Lucifer can explain."

As they continued, Eve pranced up to Asmodeus and growled. He had never gotten along with the hounds, but this time, something in her eyes told him she was trying to share something important.

"You all go on," he said. "The gates are ahead. Eve and I have something to do."

He knelt and placed a hand on her temple, feeling the softness of her fur. Matching his breath to hers, images filled his mind.

Balam in Hell with Lucifer in chains. Mick was on the table, laid out like a sacrifice. Balam stood over her watching as blood dripped into bowls underneath her wrists. The hunter had been reduced to a man chained like a dog while Astaroth sat on Lucifer's throne. Asmodeus swallowed hard as he watched these images until he saw the next few. The prophet was hung on cross and left for dead while he served as a puppet to these two filthy demons. He stared into Eve's eyes and asked her a simple question.

"Is this what happens if there is a Second War?"

No images followed—only a desperate, guttural bark.

Eve, one of Lucifer's most trusted, had made it clear: he had to stop this. He had to heal the hunter.

Asmodeus's mind raced. His plans needed to change. He could only hope Lucifer would agree. Save the hunter. Save Mick. Destroy those wretched demons.

As they approached the gates of Hell, three archangels appeared. Jophiel was among them.

"Asmodeus, we mean no harm," one said. "We bring a message for you and your hell hound."

Asmodeus looked at Jophiel, his love, and smiled. "I'm listening. What do you want of us?"

Jophiel stepped forward, handing him a golden sheet of paper covered in angelic writing. He recognized Michael's script at once. Michael was still in Hell—with Lucifer.

"Give this to Michael. We are here to help you save the hunter. When you need me, Michael will send for me, and I will come. We heard what Soul Eater said."

Asmodeus nodded. Together, they pressed on to save the hunter.

About the Author

Barb Jones is a literary force to be reckoned with, captivating readers worldwide with her best-selling and award-winning Blood Prophecy and Heaven and Hell series. An acclaimed author in the realms of supernatural thrillers and horror, she crafts gripping narratives that linger long after the last page is turned. Holding advanced degrees in Accounting, Finance, and Information Technology, Barb seamlessly blends her analytical prowess with her creative genius, resulting in stories that are both intellectually stimulating and thrillingly entertaining. With multiple accolades to her name, she writes not just for herself, but for her dedicated readers, delivering spellbinding tales that keep them on the edge of their seats. Barb Jones is not just an author; she is a master storyteller, redefining the boundaries of genre fiction.

www.thebloodprophecy.com